The Turtle Thieves

Other books by Brenda M. Spalding

The Alligator Dance

The Green Lady Inn Mystery Series
Broken Branches
Whispers in Time
Hidden Assets
The Spell Box
The Forger's Palette

Blood Orange

Honey Tree Farm – for the Love of the Beekeeper's Daughter

Bottle Alley

Deadly Bargain

A Murder for Christmas
(Short story)

The Turtle Thieves

Brenda M. Spalding

Published by
Heritage Publishing. US
Bradenton, Florida

Dedication

This work is dedicated to all the men and women who risk their lives to protect the environment and the animals that live there. The Florida Fish and Wildlife Conservation Commission Law Enforcement Officers are unsung heroes.
Protecting our native wildlife is a full-time job that requires nights, weekends, and encounters with people and animals at their best and worst. These men and women risk their lives so future generations will enjoy the wonders of nature.

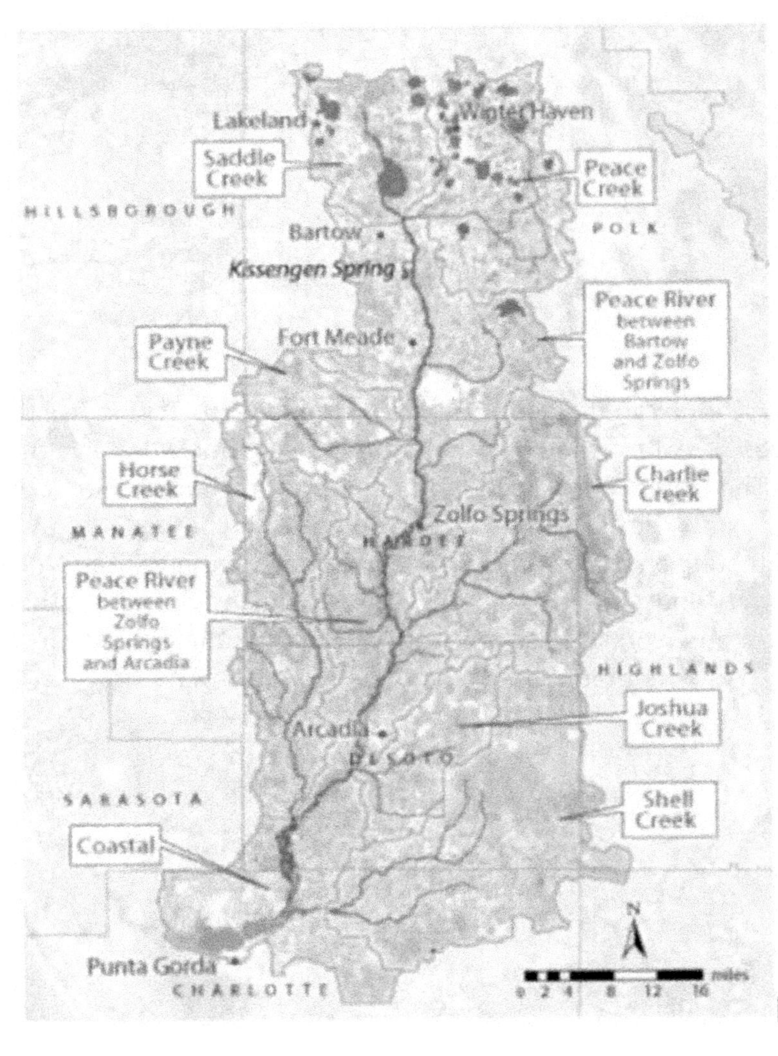

Lakeland
Winter Haven
Saddle Creek
Peace Creek
HILLSBOROUGH
POLK
Bartow
Kissengen Spring
Peace River between Bartow and Zolfo Springs
Payne Creek
Fort Meade
Horse Creek
Charlie Creek
MANATEE
Zolfo Springs
HARDEE
Peace River between Zolfo Springs and Arcadia
HIGHLANDS
Joshua Creek
Arcadia
DESOTO
SARASOTA
Shell Creek
Coastal
N
Punta Gorda
CHARLOTTE
miles
0 2 4   8   12   16

Chapter One

Hey, Dusty, what you got there?" Curtis yelled as he sat on the dock, dangling his feet into the slow-moving water. He was holding an old fishing pole in the fading light of an early summer evening, watching the occasional bat fly out of its roost high in the ancient oak trees. The boy also kept an eye on a large bull gator on the opposite bank of the Peace River. It wouldn't do to have his toes dangling if the gator decided to go looking for a snack. His ol' coon dog, Holler, was watching over the worn-out boots lying beside him, head on his paws, snoring quietly.

Dusty, his best friend, was loading some strange electric-looking stuff onto the boat tied to the county-owned dock in Pioneer Park on the corner of SR 64 and SR 17 in Zolfo Springs.

Dusty and Curtis had been friends since they were in diapers. They were also cousins.

Dusty was the handsome, smart one. He was taller by four inches and well built. His father was a bank manager, and his mom worked as a loan officer, so the family had a bit of money. Curtis struggled from grade to grade and was always the last one picked for any game. As different as they were, they would fight to protect each other.

"I've been to see Grandpa," Dusty began. "He told me how he used to catch lots a fish by using 'lectricity. He called it monkey fishing. Him and a bunch of his buddies would go out on a night like this and catch enough fish to have a big ol' fish fry for everyone."

"How can you use 'lectricity to catch fish?" Curtis wondered. "Our Uncle Wade, you remember him, told me how he used dynamite for fishing until Harold Hunsaker blew off two of his fingers." The boy chuckled.

Curtis jumped. "Shit." Feeling a tug on his line. Finally, a fish was on his hook. He reeled the line in, hoping for a giant fat catfish for dinner. He was so excited that he almost stepped off the dock's edge.

Dusty snickered, shaking his head and laughing at his cousin as he continued to load the small two-person aluminum boat.

"Damn it all to hell," Curtis swore. The small fish dangling at the end of his line was a little bluegill. Not the monster catfish he was hoping for. He'd need a dozen more of these tiddlers to make a meal. His mom would not be pleased if all he brought home was one lousy sunfish.

Disgusted, Curtis threw the fish back and dropped his rod on the deck, strolling over to see what Curtis had going on. "So, tell me about this fishing with 'lectricity."

"Grandpa took me to this shed out back o' his house, and he showed me this box o' stuff. There was an ol' phone, and this thing he called a magneto. He said it's like a generator. You hook the phone up to the magneto and throw this here cable in the water."

"Don't it kill the fish?" Curtis was busy inspecting the things Dusty loaded in the boat. He couldn't wait to try it out and see it work.

"Nah, you adjust the current. Grandpa says you got to be careful. You only want to tickle 'em, so they raise to the surface. If the current is too strong, they swim away, and you don't get any. He told me how to use it."

Dusty continued to stow the gear away under the seats of the boat, covering it with an oilcloth.

"When you gonna do this? Can I come, Dusty? Can I?" Curtis shifted from one bare foot to the other, his hands in the pockets of his well-worn bib overalls, tossing his head to get his honey-colored hair out of his eyes.

"I'm fixing to take off now. You have to leave Holler. He might get excited and tip the boat over."

"I'm comin'," Curtis jumped into the boat and told Holler to stay put. Holler put on a sad face and lay down. The old dog was OK not going in the boat when they went fishing. It upset his stomach.

The sun was setting while Dusty put the equipment together, but a full moon was rising to light the river in a soft glow. An Eastern indigo snake slithered from its hiding place in the palmettos to begin hunting as bats left their roost high in oaks. Silver minnows danced at the water's edge.

"This thing gets going; you stay on the seat. You stand on the bottom of the boat in your bare feet, and you'll be dancing along with the fish," Dusty couldn't help enjoying the look of anxiety and fear on Curtis's face.

The stars were just starting to peek out of the darkening sky as Dusty threw the cable into the shallow dark water for the first time and turned on the juice. A hum filled the air around them. The water vibrated, and fish began to dance to the surface.

"You did it, Dusty. The fish are dancing to your tune." Curtis was so excited. He grabbed a long-handled net and started to scoop fish into the boat. Bluegill, redear sunfish, and even a couple good size largemouth bass floated to the surface. Slipping off the seat, he put a foot down on the metal bottom of the boat to balance himself. Curtis felt a healthy zing go through his whole body, making his hair stand on end.

"Wow, I feel sorry for them fish," Curtis said as he quickly scrabbled back onto the bench seat, still feeling his insides vibrate.

Suddenly from the bank came a flash of light, stunning the boys. They shielded their eyes, trying to see who it was.

"Ah, crap," Dusty cursed, turning down the current.

"Who's that?" Curtis whispered, trying to hide behind Dusty.

"That's the man that's gonna put us in jail."

"Why's he gonna put us in jail, Dusty?"

"Because monkey fishing is against the law, dummy."

"You never said nothing about that," Curtis cried. "An, don't call me dummy."

Chapter Two

Pulling his Florida Fish and Wildlife vehicle off the road behind a stand of live oak trees dripping with Spanish moss, Officer Seth Grayson had stopped to watch a couple of young boys at a rickety wooden dock and boat ramp. One of them had pushed a rusty old johnboat into the water.

Seth eased himself closer through the pine trees and prickly palmettos to listen to what the boys were saying. Seeing youngsters enjoying the water and fishing was the fun part of his job. It brought back memories of his childhood growing up on the Seminole Indian reservation in Tampa, Hillsborough County. It was sad to see the big Hard Rock Casino changing the way of life he had enjoyed as a kid.

His father would often take him to visit cousins on the Big Cypress Reservation three hours south down near the Everglades. Their hunting trips inspired his love of the land and the wildlife that lived there.

The Peace River near Arcadia was part of his patrol area. After training to be a Florida Fish and Wildlife Law Enforcement Officer, he partnered with other officers to fine-tune his training. Seth finally earned the badge and had his own patrol. His area overlapped with Sarasota, Manatee, Desoto, and Hardee counties in Southwest Florida. It was challenging, and he never knew what the day or night might bring. Today was no exception.

It was definitely different from working as a park ranger in the

Manasota State Park, where he met Florida Fish and Wildlife Officer Liz Corday, and she introduced him to the work of the FWC. Alligator egg poachers targeted the park a dozen miles south in Sarasota County. As they chased the poachers, he learned about the valuable work the FWC does. Now he was in law enforcement, sharing his heart and his home with a woman who loved the life as much as he did.

Chapter Three

Curtis sat down heavily on the boat seat, his eyes wide and filling with tears. "I can't go to jail, Dusty. My ma will tan my hide."

The officer walked down the leaf-littered bank to the water's edge.

"Pull that boat over here, boys," Seth called out across the water. The evening was fully dark now, and the only light was the quarter moon above. An owl hooted high above in the trees, waking to start its night hunting. The sound of its dinner rustled in the undergrowth.

Dusty and Curtis paddled their way to the riverbank. Sitting in the boat, they looked up into the stern face of the Florida Fish and Wildlife Commission Officer.

"Hi, boys. I'm Officer Seth Grayson, and what you are doing is highly illegal."

Seth pulled the boat up on the bank and looked at the equipment and all the fish they had managed to catch.

"How old are you, boys?"

"We're thirteen, sir," Dusty answered for both of them.

"And who told you about monkey fishing and gave you this equipment?"

"My grandpa did, officer."

"Well, I want you to get back to the dock and tie up your boat. I'll meet you there. We'll call your parents and have a long talk about what you've been up to," Seth said, letting go of the battered and worn johnboat.

He watched one of the boys start the two-stroke trolling motor and aim for the dock.

In the faint light from the moon, Seth saw maybe a half dozen little turtle tracks on the sandy bank. The hatching season was well underway in late spring. If only the river could remain true to its name. Phosphate mining runoff, agricultural waste, and other pollution from the surrounding areas were plaguing the once-pristine river.

Seth's thoughts returned to the two boys as he climbed into his vehicle. Shaking his head, he had to laugh at their antics. Seth had heard stories about monkey fishing along the rivers. But he thought it was just some of the older officers pulling his leg. They told him it was an old poacher's trick. He could only believe that Dusty's grandpa had filled his head with stories of the good ol' days.

The officer looked forward to meeting Grandpa. Seth felt that the older man might have gotten himself arrested a time or two. There was a new generation of poachers coming along. He hoped he could turn these two away from the life before he had to arrest them as well in a few years.

Chapter Four

Seth called in the report as he drove around to meet up with his young poachers. The boat ramp looked like the Fourth of July with flashing blue lights from two more FWC patrol vehicles. He recognized his girlfriend, Officer Liz Corday, in the glow of the headlights as she climbed out of one of the trucks

Officer Jessup, a new trainee, watched over Dusty and Curtis as they sat on one of the picnic benches. Jessup usually worked with different partners for the experience. This evening he was on his own.

"Hey, Chief, you brought in a couple of big-time poachers there." Liz laughed as she caught up with Seth in the parking lot.

"They all start somewhere. I hope we can put the fear of God into these two, so they'll think twice about doing something like this again. Care to play along?"

"Sure, let's go," Liz said, smiling. She was up for playing good cop, bad cop.

Liz and Seth walked up to the two young cousins. "What are your names, boys?" Seth asked.

"My name is Dusty Stirling. This is my cousin Curtis Dunbar; his dog's name is Holler. Our grandpa is Hap Dunbar,"

"Well, what have you got to say for yourselves?" Seth said, trying to use his most authoritative and frightening voice. Liz ducked her head behind Seth's back to hide her giggle

Curtis's face showed traces of white where the tears had washed away the dirt of the day's play. Holler had his big head across the young boy's lap, looking as sad as the boy felt.

Dusty spoke up first., "I didn't know it was bad. It just looked like a bit of fun. We only wanted to tickle 'em fish into the boat, is all." The boy slumped with his head down, busy studying his dirty fingernails. "My grandpa did say to watch out for you guys. Guess we didn't watch out so good."

"I want to have a word with your grandpa," Liz interjected and sat beside the boys. The man must have known it was illegal if their grandfather had warned the boys. What kind of example was that setting for two impressionable kids? Liz was upset Hap Dunbar would do that to his grandsons.

"I'm going to write you a warning because of your age. It will still go on your record if you decide to do something like this again," Seth told the youngsters, bracing his boot on the bench to write the warning ticket on his knee.

"We are going to have to meet with your grandpa. He should know better than to tell you how to break the law," Liz said, standing erect with her hand on her gun, hoping to get her message across.

Seth turned to the younger officer, "Officer Jessup will take you boys home. He'll explain to your parents about the warning. They can call if they have any questions. Officer Corday or I will be around to speak with your grandpa in the morning. Give us his address and his phone number.

Liz and Seth watched Officer Jessup load up Dusty, Curtis, and Holler for the trip back to their parents in Nocatee, just south of Zolfo Springs, two communities with deep old Florida Cracker roots.

Curtis stopped, turning back, his head tilted to the side in thought.

"Can I ask you something, officer?"

"Sure, let's have it," Seth said.

Curtis looked at his feet, scratching Holler behind his ears., "The lady officer called you Chief, and you look like the Indians in our schoolbooks. We're studying the Florida Indians. Are you one of those?"

"Yes, I am, Curtis. I'm a Seminole Indian. Maybe you could use your school library to look up some information on the Seminoles. The Indians were here in Florida long before the white man arrived."

"Wow," Curtis stared at the striking man before him.

Seth was almost six feet. Tall for a Seminole. His collar-length hair was the blue-black of a raven's wing. Seth's gray-green eyes were a gift from a white ancestor. Two parallel lines on his cheek from a snake bite in his youth only made him more mysterious.

"Thanks, officer," Curtis said.

Seth helped to usher Holler into the waiting FWC vehicle.

Curtis waved from the FWC truck as it drove away.

"That was fun," Liz said solemnly.

"It rattles me when people who should know better teach youngsters how to do something against the law."

"I know how you feel. It makes me angry too. We'll see what Grandpa Dunbar has to say in the morning."

Chapter Five

It was after 8 p.m. when Liz and Seth finally arrived at their home in Sarasota near the Manasota State Park, tired and hungry.

Liz yawned, walking up the porch steps. "Let's have an early night. I'm beat."

"Me too," Seth agreed. Opening the kitchen door, he was almost knocked off his feet by his dog, Nokosi. The dog started as a small ball of fur and kept growing. He was given the dog by a cousin four years ago. The puppy was of unknown parentage when found on the side of the road. For some reason, the cousin decided that Seth needed the dog and deposited him on Seth's doorstep. Seth named him Nokosi, Seminole for bear.

"Hey there. Did you think I forgot about you?" Seth knelt to take the big dog's head in his hands and give him a hug and scratch. The dog's look of pure ecstasy made Liz laugh.

"You shower first. I'll feed our friend here and see what's in the fridge." Liz said.

"You're an angel." Seth kissed Liz lightly and went down the hall to shower and change. Seth and Liz began living together while working on an alligator poaching case.

Seth leaned his head against the tiles and let the warm water wash over him as he remembered how lucky he was to have Liz in his life.

It was a rocky beginning at first. Liz had some emotional baggage from an earlier relationship, and Seth was trying to figure out where he fit in life as a non-traditional Seminole.

Liz rattled around in the kitchen, opening the bag of food and a can for Nokosi.

Liz had a special place in her heart for the big dog. He had saved her life a couple times when alligator egg poachers were trying to scare her away from investigating their illegal activities.

The dog stopped her entering her truck, where the poachers left a present of a large rattler. He warned her when the poachers came to the house, leaving a dead raccoon on the hood of her truck.

Searching through the fridge, Liz came up with enough salad and an omelet for their supper. She quickly put the mixture together before Seth walked into the kitchen dressed in baggy jogging pants and a tee-shirt, toweling his damp shoulder-length black hair.

Liz put her arms around Seth, resting her head on his chest, "Mmm, you smell good."

"It's the stuff you gave me for Christmas."

"It's nice. I'll be quick. We can eat soon." Liz rushed away.

Seth poured two glasses of iced tea and sat at the kitchen table. Nokosi came and rested his head in Seth's lap.

"Miss me today?"

He absently stroked the dog's head, letting his thoughts wander back to how he met Liz; now, she was living with him in Sarasota. Liz still had her condo in Tampa and was thinking of selling it, but something was holding her back.

"Penny for your thoughts," Liz said, sliding into Seth's lap.

"Just thinking about how lucky I am." Seth nuzzled her neck. She leaned into him, relaxing.

"Eat now. Get lucky later," Liz said, pushing up and bringing together the ingredients for their supper.

After their meal, they took their coffee to the living area. Their home was a cozy place with a large front and back porch. Seth had several pieces of Seminole art and pottery arranged around the living room. A comfy couch draped with a colorful Indian blanket faced the fireplace. Cuddled up on the sofa, Liz asked Seth, "You want me to go with you tomorrow?"

"Oh, I think I can handle one old poacher and a couple young kids."

"What are your plans for tomorrow?"

"I have to go in to see Captain Jacobs. There have been some reports of turtle smuggling in the area," Liz said.

"I'm still new at this. Why smuggle turtles?" Seth asked. All the training in the world could not keep up with the illegal way criminals would try to profit from wildlife. FWC agents had to be constantly on the lookout and learning about the job.

"Native Florida turtles are disappearing at an alarming rate. There was a case recently where turtles were trafficked for $300 each, then sold retail in the Asian markets, Singapore, Hong Kong, and Tokyo, for $10,000. That investigation was down south in Lee County, but we have to keep an eye open," Liz said.

"When I was watching those kids tonight, I saw a lot of little turtle tracks on the banks," Seth said.

"They'll be hatching from now through the Fall. Now is when we have to watch out and keep those little guys safe. I'll try doing some more research on it and see what I can find," Liz said, picking up the cups and taking them into the kitchen while Seth let Nokosi out to do his business one last time.

Seth stood on the steps listening to the night sounds of the cicadas buzzing in the trees, watching as a couple bats swept across the full moon, chasing mosquitoes. Liz came up and wrapped her arms around him.

"Come in before the bugs eat you alive."

"It's just so peaceful. I love it here." Seth turned in her arms, encircling her and dipping his head to take her lips with his, delving deep, yearning for more. "I love having you here with me. I never thought I could be this happy."

Liz fingered the silver snake on a chain that Seth had given her a while ago. Liz wondered if she was ready to take the next step in their relationship and get engaged to be married. Yet, she still worried and asked herself, was she prepared for that kind of commitment?

Chapter Six

Liz was up and dressed early, anxious to beat Tampa's traffic, when Seth walked into the kitchen. Her trips to her condo were less and less frequent. She only went to Tampa when she had to meet with Captain Jacobs at his office.

"You were tossing and turning last night. Is everything alright?" Seth drew Liz to him, putting his arms around her.

"It's my mom," Liz said. "She called to say she's coming to Tampa for a visit. I haven't seen her in years. We talk on the phone a couple times a year. You know, Christmas and other holidays."

Seth knew Liz's relationship with her mother was strained since her parents divorced several years ago. Her mother had not often reached out to Liz, and their conversations were always short and to the point.

Seth could tell Liz was holding something back. "What are you not telling me?"

Liz pulled away and went to look out the window over the kitchen sink. Her back to Seth, she said, "It's more than that."

"You better tell me."

"She doesn't know about my job."

"She doesn't know you work for the FWC?"

"She thinks I work in an office for the FWC as an admin assistant pushing papers around."

"You're telling me she doesn't know you run around catching

poachers, almost getting eaten by alligators, and carrying a big 'ol Glock?" Seth tried to hide a grimace and shook his head in disbelief. Liz had gotten herself into quite a mess this time.

"There's more."

"Do I want to know?" Seth wondered what could be so bad about not having the job her mother thought she had.

It suddenly came to him. "You haven't told her about us yet?"

"Mom doesn't know I'm living with anyone." Liz felt her legs give out. She sat in one of the kitchen chairs. Unsure how Seth would take the news that he didn't exist to her mother.

"Liz, we've been together for over two years." Seth could feel his temper rising as he tried to digest what Liz was telling him.

"She knows I'm dating someone, but that's all I've told her."

"So basically, your mother knows absolutely nothing about me? Or our life together?"

"I've tried to tell her, but she has this way of telling me how she wants me to live my life."

Tears ran down Liz's cheeks when the kitchen door slammed.

Chapter Seven

Seth tried to calm down and get his mind on the job as he drove up SR 17 to meet Dusty and Curtis's grandfather Hap Dunbar. He expected the worst from this old cracker.

Following GPS directions, he arrived at a run-down single-wide trailer at the end of a dirt road. Mr. Dunbar's property backed up to a large wildlife park. The northern border of the park was the Peace River. The Hardee County Wildlife Refuge and the Pioneer Park Museum were included in the park. The area was a favorite of locals and visitors for the boat ramp and picnic areas.

Pulling in, Seth saw a yard littered with old pieces of car parts, farm equipment, and other useless junk.

Mr. Dunbar came out the door of the trailer as Seth pulled in. Right behind him were two towheaded little girls. They appeared to be about five and seven.

"Hi, are you Mr. Dunbar.?" Seth asked, seeing an older man in his sixties wearing a worn and faded work shirt and jeans that had seen better days. The man's face showed years of struggle to survive any way he could.

"Yeah, I'm Hap Dunbar. These are my granddaughters, Lucy and Melinda. What does the FWC want with me? I ain't been doing nothing."

"My name is Officer Seth Grayson. I came to talk to you about the equipment you gave to your grandson, Dusty."

"Yeah, I gave him some old junk. What of it?" Dunbar's stance and manner were belligerent and defensive.

Seth took notice and tried to defuse the situation.

"I'm not trying to jack anyone up for anything," Seth said. "I found Dusty and Curtis out monkey fishing on the Peace River last night. I looked up your record and found that you and the FWC have met before. I know that you know that monkey fishing is illegal."

That softened Dunbar up a bit.

"Yeah, I have a nodding acquaintance with you guys."

His shoulders dropped when he asked, "Did you arrest my grandsons?"

"No. I let both boys off with a warning and confiscated the equipment. I imagine their parents were none too happy seeing them brought home in an FWC patrol truck last night."

"No, I guess not. Dusty's dad is a stuck-up son of a bitch. My daughter Mary married up with that one, but he likes to throw it around. My other daughter, Curtis's mother, Lorraine, tries, but her husband is away too much, and she works too hard."

"I can understand, but it's no excuse. You, of all people, should know better."

"I was just hoping to give the boys a bit of fun, is all. They like hearing stories from the old days, back before all the developments and traffic took all the woods and wildlife away. And all the rules you guys came up with." Dunbar spat out the last bit.

"I know what you mean, but no more poaching stories. Teach them how to enjoy nature and save it for their own children."

Seth looked at the young girls playing with something in a small plastic wading pool under an oak tree. He wandered over to take a look and was shocked to see the pool contained at least thirty baby turtles of different species, most on the endangered list.

Chapter Eight

"What have you got here, girls?" Seth asked them.

Dunbar had followed Seth and stood behind the officer, shaking his head and scowling with his hands deep in his worn-out jeans pockets.

"We have a business," the younger one, Lucy, told him excitedly.

"Yeah, Grandpa says we're 'pernures. We make one dollar for every turtle we put in the pool." Melinda said.

"Then Momma takes us to the Dollar Tree. We get to spend half of it, and Momma gets to have the rest. We don't think that fair, but she says it is because she feeds us." The little girls were so proud and happy to show off their business.

Seth took off his hat, ran his hands through his hair, and stared at the sky for a minute. He couldn't believe what he was hearing.

"Mr. Dunbar, we need to talk some more," Seth said.

"Shit, man, what the hell is the matter now?" Dunbar was getting aggravated again, stomping around and kicking at the dirt.

"I'm afraid there is. Some of Florida's turtles are endangered and taking them from the wild is illegal. There are rules on how many you can take. I don't want you to pay expensive fines of a couple hundred dollars for each turtle or even go to jail."

"That's bull. There's plenty of them critters out there," Dunbar shouted, gesturing to the woods and the park down by the river beyond his house.

"Mr. Dunbar, great you are trying to help your family out, but the girls can't keep the turtles. It's illegal. They must put the turtles back close to where they found them."

Dunbar was furious, shaking his head and tight-lipped; he stood there with his arms across his chest. His stance defiant.

"This is crazy. Those little girls ain't doing no harm."

"Mr. Dunbar, it's against the law for the girls to keep the turtles. They must be released back to where they found them." Seth knew he was dealing with an old-school poacher and hoped he was getting through to him.

"I'll be back in a couple of days to check. In the meantime, I'm issuing you a warning for keeping endangered wildlife." Seth wrote out the warning on the hood of his truck and handed it to the older man.

Taking the piece of paper from Seth, Dunbar crunched it up and shoved it in his pocket.

"This is bullshit. It's just a few turtles," the man raged.

Seth took out his mobile phone and took pictures of the turtles in the pool. He also wrote down the species in his notebook. That would help later if Dunbar did not heed the warning.

Driving away, Seth watched Dunbar talking to his two granddaughters, watching the children starting to argue and cry over the turtles.

Turning back to SR 17 and heading out on patrol, Seth called Captain Jacobs and told him about Dunbar and the turtles. He said that he would send in a full written report later.

Captain Jacobs told Seth that turtle trafficking was becoming a big concern in some states. Most people knew that sea turtles were endangered, but few knew freshwater turtles were also in peril.

The rest of the day was relatively peaceful. He checked some fishing licenses and issued a couple of warnings. The only disturbing call came from a bee farm east of Arcadia about a bear disturbing his hives. Seth said he would check on it as soon as possible.

Heading home and getting closer to Sarasota, Seth wondered what might be waiting for him there. This morning was the first time Liz and he had had a real bust-up, and it bothered him that they had not been able to talk it out. He should have tried to talk with Liz, but he was so angry, thinking Liz didn't tell her mother about their relationship because he was Seminole.

Chapter Nine

The sun was setting when Seth pulled into his yard in Sarasota. His heart sank when he didn't see Liz's FWC truck parked in its usual spot under the old oak tree.

"Well, I see at least you still love me," Seth said, greeting Nokosi, who almost knocked him over. Sitting on the floor with the dog trying to climb in his lap, Seth wondered if things were over between him and Liz. "Not if I can help it," he said to Nokosi as he pushed himself up.

After hanging up his hat and taking off his gun belt, Seth went to the fridge for a cold beer and found a note from Liz sitting on the six-pack.

> *Hi Chief,*
> *Sorry about this morning. My mother has not been involved in my life for many years, and our relationship is strange. For some reason, she wants to connect, and it scares me.*
> *She has always tried to control my life, and I'm afraid she is doing it again.*
> *I'm meeting her at my condo in Tampa for a couple of days. I promise to tell her all about my job and us.*
> *I love you very much and will explain more when I see you.*
> *Liz.*

Seth read the note over a couple times and finally felt better. He would give Liz a few days to deal with her mother, and then they would talk about things.

After digging through the fridge, Seth found enough to put a meal together. He fed Nokosi and had dinner while searching on the internet for the turtles he had seen in the pool at Dunbar's place that day.

Seth refined the list of the turtles he had seen and sent a copy of the photo he had taken to Captain Jacobs along with his report.

There were rules and limits for taking turtles from the wild. Little Lucy and Melinda had way too many turtles in their pool.

There were rules on the number of turtles someone was allowed to possess and permits to be applied for; some species were illegal to possess under any conditions.

Taking a beer with him, Seth sat on the porch and watched Nokosi sniffing around, looking for a place to do his thing. He thought about how lonely it was without Liz sitting on the rocker beside him. He wondered how she was getting on with her mother and hoped Liz would be strong enough to deal with whatever the problem was between them.

Chapter Ten

Liz's mother finished unpacking her few things in the spare bedroom while Liz wondered how she would begin to tell her mother about her life with the FWC and, more importantly, her life with Seth.

Her mother had always been a dominating force and was one of the main reasons her parents divorced. Nothing Liz did was ever right or good enough for her mother.

Constance Corday was from a prominent Tallahassee family and made sure everyone knew it. How or why her parents ever got together in the first place was a mystery to her. Her parents came from different worlds and wanted different things out of life. She knew they met in college but not the details. Her dad came from central Florida and grew up hunting and camping. He tried to live the life her mother wanted, but was not happy.

Liz knew Seth's world was different from hers, but they both wanted the same things.

Sitting down to a Chinese takeaway, Liz and her mother exchanged pleasant talks about the weather and the food. There was obvious tension they were trying to cover up. It was not a friendly mother-and-daughter chat.

"I guess you don't have much time to cook?" Constance said, pushing her sweet and sour chicken around on her plate.

"No, I don't cook very often. I'm usually not here much." Liz was afraid of this conversation, pushing her own meal around with her chopsticks. She delayed by sipping her wine and hoped to dodge what might be coming. Liz could face armed poachers, no problem, but her mother scared the shit out of her.

"What do you mean, you're not here much? You're an administrative assistant for the state. You must have regular hours. Oh, are you too busy dating again? That's wonderful!" Constance gushed. "You must tell me all about him. I bet he's some government official. It's about time you met someone of quality to settle down with."

"Mom, I'm not an administrative assistant. I've tried to tell you that several times, but you don't listen. I'm an agent for the Florida Fish and Wildlife Conservation Commission."

"That's fine, darling. It's still a government position. So, you're a secretary, is that it?"

Liz started to clear the dishes, bracing herself for what might be a heated argument with her mother.

"I'm in law enforcement, Mom. I wear a badge and carry a gun. I catch bad guys. You know, hunters breaking the law, poachers, wildlife traffickers. They kill animals illegally and sometimes people that try to stop them." Constance sat in stunned silence. After a few minutes, she got up and brought her plate to the sink.

"You have got to be kidding. I blame your father for this. He always took you to see his brother, Dan, that policeman. Dan told you all those horrible stories. Your father took you camping and all that disgusting outdoor stuff with the bugs and other stuff. They warped your mind."

Liz turned to face her mother, "Mom, it's what I love. I enjoy what I do. It's different every day. I couldn't stand being cooped up in an office all day."

"How can you possibly hope to meet the right man to settle down with while carrying a gun? You're running around in the woods. Is that a place to find a respectable husband?"

Liz got up and stepped to the window overlooking the large pond behind her building. A great blue heron was standing at the water's edge, hoping for an evening meal.

"Mom, it may surprise you that I have made my choices because they make me happy, not because they piss you off." Liz was angry and trying to control her anger. Gritting her teeth and clenching her fists, she stared out the window. "I'm not you. I don't want the same things you do."

Constance joined her daughter at the window, lifting her hands but hesitating to put her arms around Liz's shoulders. She placed them gently on Liz's shoulders.

"Don't you want to get married and have a nice house and children?" Constance said, looking at their reflections in the window.

"Yes, but I'm in no hurry."

"Come back to Tallahassee with me. I can introduce you to several eligible bachelors at my country club. I know a promising young heart surgeon who would be perfect for you."

Liz took a breath to control herself., "You are not listening. I don't want a heart surgeon. I don't want a country club life."

Liz moved to put the couch between herself and her mother. "I have someone in my life who I love."

Constance almost screamed, "You're not gay, are you?"

"Would that be so bad if I were, Mom? But no, I'm not," Liz said. She fingered the silver snake pendant around her neck that Seth had given her. "I live with a man. His name is Seth Grayson. He's also with the Florida Fish and Wildlife Commission."

"I think I need to go lay down." Constance walked slowly back to her room. Her daughter's revelations were swirling in her mind.

Liz sank down on a chair. *This is not going well. Seth, I miss you. Mom hasn't even heard the rest of it.*

Chapter Eleven

Hap Dunbar watched a sleek black Jeep SUV pull into his yard; he was glad his granddaughters were not here today. Hap figured today would not end well.

After the FWC officer's visit, Hap returned all the turtles to the park behind his house. His granddaughters had cried and fussed about it something awful, but he didn't want any trouble from the FWC, resulting in a considerable fine he couldn't afford or going to jail.

As two men climbed out of the SUV, Hap wondered if he should have made a different decision.

"Hello, Mr. Dunbar. How's it going today?" The shorter of the two men, aged about forty, said. The man spoke perfect English but with a Chinese accent. He was dressed in a flowery cotton short-sleeve shirt, expensive dress pants, and shiny leather shoes.

His tone was intimidating while trying to sound friendly, like a cat toying with a mouse.

"I'm fine. You fellas lost? You're not from around these parts." After a beat, Hap asked, "Eh, how do you know my name?" Hap was getting a very uneasy feeling.

The larger of the two men, an inch or two over six feet, was circling around behind him. Hap tried to keep him in his field of vision but focused on the man in front of him.

"My name is Phan Pen. I work for a certain organization in Singapore. You have been doing business with my associate Matt

Troyer. I believe you have a deal to deliver turtles to him. He had an unfortunate accident, and I'm here to collect for him today."

Dunbar stonewalled, "I'm not doing that anymore. Not since I had a visit from a Florida Fish and Wildlife officer. He said it's illegal to take the turtles from the wild. Some of them are endangered. I could go to jail if I get caught with turtles again. I've had some run-ins with those guys before. They don't play around, and I can't afford to get into any more trouble."

"Mr. Dunbar, I don't care what the officer said," Pen said, spitting the words out. "I want those turtles. I have buyers lined up waiting for them." All friendliness had left, and his cruel stance enforced his intent to get what he wanted.

"You have got to be kidding me. I'm not going to jail for you or anyone. Mr. Troyer never said anything about it being illegal."

Hap could feel the man behind him getting closer, making the hair on the back of his neck stand up. Did he have a gun at his back?

"I told you I couldn't do it anymore. I wish I could help you fellas out, but I'm not doing anything that will put me in jail. I have my family to think about. I take care of my little granddaughters." Hap could feel the big man brush up against his back.

"Mr. Pen wants those turtles. You don't want anything to happen to your little granddaughters, do you?" the man whispered in Hap's ear. "Not honoring a deal has consequences."

"Leave them out of this," Hap shouted, trying to step away, fear making his stomach lurch.

"My associate, Jarod, there will have to convince you to cooperate. If you do not produce fifty turtles by the time I return, your granddaughters will suffer the consequences."

"Convince Mr. Dunbar for me, Jarod." Pen turned and walked back to the Jeep, waving casually over his shoulder.

Chapter Twelve

Approaching the Dunbar place, Seth noticed that the children's pool was not in the front yard. He was pleased. Maybe Hap and his granddaughters had put the turtles back where they belonged.

Seth walked up the creaky wooden steps to the trailer's front door, and before he could knock, Hap Dunbar threw it open.

Hap stood there glaring at Seth. He had an angry black eye, a split lip, and a possible broken nose. The old man bent over in pain and shouted, "What the hell do you want?"

"Mr. Dunbar, who did this to you?"

"A lot you care."

"I do care. Someone beat the shit out of you, and I want to know who and why." Seth was furious that anyone would do this to an old man. "Look, I want to help. Can we talk about this?"

"No, they said they will come after my granddaughters if I do. I can't risk that." Dunbar turned to go back inside. Seth put his hand on the man's bony shoulder and stopped him, turning him back around. A crazy thought crossed his mind.

"Mr. Dunbar, does this have anything to do with the turtles I saw the other day?"

"Oh, you are one smart Indian, ain't ya?"

"It's got nothing to do with my being an Indian. The FWC has reports of turtle trafficking in Lee County, outside of Ft Myers. I guess it got too hot for them down there, so they moved up here. You got caught up in a bad situation."

"Ya think?" Dunbar lifted his craggy face.

"If you help us out here, we can help you. These traffickers are not going to stop. Talk to me. What did they say?"

Dunbar gave up; his shoulders slumped as he pushed past Seth, walking slowly down the steps to a couple plastic chairs set out around a firepit. Dropping his head in his hands, he stared into the smoking embers before continuing.

"They're coming back, and I need fifty turtles for them or else. I don't want to know what *or else* means."

Seth sat in the other chair, his hands clasped between his knees. He had to help this man and catch this group of traffickers. He wished he had Liz to talk to. She had several more years of experience and would have an idea about what to do.

"Leave it with me, Mr. Dunbar. I'll call my captain and see what he suggests we do. I'm not going to let you handle this alone. Do you want to see a doctor? You seem to be in quite a bit of pain. You might have some damaged ribs."

"No, but thanks for asking. I'll manage."

Chapter Thirteen

Seth ran from the shower to answer his phone. Tripping over Nokosi, he picked it up and was happy to see Liz's ID on the readout. "Hey, I'm so glad you called, sweetheart. How's it going with your mother? Or should I ask?" Seth said, trying to wrap a towel around his waist with one hand.

"Seth, it's a disaster. She just doesn't get it. I told her I'm in law enforcement with the FWC, and she almost blew a gasket."

Liz stopped to blow her nose. Seth could tell she was crying and wanted to hold her in his arms and make it all better.

"At least she knows now."

"She wanted to take me back to Tallahassee so I could meet a promising young surgeon or another eligible man at her country club."

"Oh boy, what did you say to that?" Seth asked, sitting quickly on the couch. He was afraid she might say she was going, yet hoped she would stand her ground.

"You would be proud of me. I told my mom I was living with a man who also worked for the FWC. She didn't give me a chance to tell her more. I wanted to tell her about you, but she stormed out of the room. I wanted to tell her how much I love you and want to be with you."

"Sweetheart, I am immensely proud of you. I love you too, very much. We can talk more about this when I see you. Which I hope will be soon. I miss you. By the way, Officer Corday, I also need help with these turtle traffickers."

Liz laughed. "There's always an ulterior motive with you, isn't there?"

"Hey, it's lonely here without you. Nokosi misses you too."

"Ok, Chief, Mom will probably head back to Tallahassee, and I can come home. Home sounds so good. One last thing, I made up my mind. I'm selling the damn condo."

Chapter Fourteen

Constance gave Liz the silent treatment over coffee in the morning.

"Mom, this is ridiculous. We need to talk about this," Liz said, standing in her tiny kitchen dressed in her FWC uniform with her Glock strapped to her hip.

"I'm looking at my daughter standing there with a gun, and I'm ridiculous?" Constance shot back.

"It's part of my job, Mom. Why don't you come with me today? Do a ride-along. See what I do in a day. I can clear it with my captain. It might give you a different perspective." Liz wanted her mother's approval more than anything but held out little hope that she could convince the country club queen to accompany her. Liz held her breath waiting, shifting from foot to foot, while Constance finished her coffee without a word.

"Ok, I'll do it. What does one wear on a ride-along?"

"Mom, wear whatever you want. I know you don't own blue jeans, but long pants and low-heeled shoes would be best. I never know where I'm going or what I might do."

Liz could only hope that her day would be about expired fishing licenses or injured wildlife that needed transporting to a wildlife rescue.

Maybe they would find a way to talk, and Liz would finally have the opportunity to tell her mother about Seth, the whole story about Seth. She knew her mother would not understand, but Liz had to convince her to stay out of her life and let her live it her way.

Liz called the captain to get permission for her mother to ride with her. Then she waited while her mom took ages picking out what to wear. Constance Corday had to have the right coordinated outfit for an FWC ride-along.

Chapter Fifteen

"Come on, Holler. What have you got there? I sure hope it ain't some stinky dead thing. The last time you rolled in somethin', it stunk up the whole house," Curtis shouted to his old Bloodhound. "Momma will not let you in the house again until I give you a bath. Hell, she might even make me take one."

The dog had a habit of finding the most disgusting things as Curtis, and his cousin Dusty roamed the park along the Peace River. The cousins had been out all morning tramping through the woods exploring and were tired, hungry, and thirsty. Long ago, they had found ways to avoid paying the daily admission fee and explore the reserve and the river running beside it.

"What does that stupid dog have this time?" Dusty called out, running to catch up to Curtis and Holler.

"He ain't stupid. He's just curious, is all," Curtis said, defending his precious pet.

What Dusty saw stopped him in his tracks. "Aw shit," Dusty whispered, taking off his ball cap and running his hands through his dark blond hair.

Curtis struggled to hold Holler back.

Stretched out and partially covered with debris lay a dead body. A man had been shot execution-style. Flies were gathering around the black and bloody hole in the back of his skull. A sticky pool of dried blood flowed onto the leaf-covered ground around the man's head.

"We need to tell someone," Curtis said.

"Yeah, but who?"

"I got the number for that wildlife lady. Let's call her. She'll know what to do." Curtis sat on the ground, his arms around his dog, tears running down his face. He had never seen a dead body before. Definitely, never someone had been killed in such a brutal manner.

"We gotta go to Joe's and call 'er," Curtis mumbled, his mouth pressed against Holler's large head.

Dusty nodded and reached out to help his cousin stand. "Come on. Let's call that lady cop of yours."

The two boys hiked to the main road and down to Joe's Bait Shop on SR 17. Joe Harris was standing behind the counter when the boys pushed through the door. "What's up? You look a bit frazzled."

"You gotta help us, Joe. We found a dead body in the park. He's got a big hole in his head. We gotta call this FWC lady. She'll know what to do." Curtis handed him Liz's card and leaned against the counter, his eyes pleading for help. Dusty stood behind him, hands on his cousin's shoulders for support and comfort.

Joe knew they were talking about Pioneer Park, not far from his bait shop. It was a 240-acre preserve on the edge of Zolfo Springs. Hardee County owned the park with the Department of Environmental Protection cooperation. A favorite picnic and hiking spot, it retained the isolation and feel of old Florida.

Joe looked over the tattered business card Curtis handed him. "When are you guys gonna get a cell phone?" Joe said, stepping away and calling the agent's number on the card.

"Dusty, we're thirteen; how can we afford one of those fancy phones?" Curtis asked his cousin.

"I can sell you a cheep one for $29."

"My dad says maybe when I can pay for it myself," Dusty said.

"I don't know. Maybe some lucky kids do have 'em," Curtis said, looking at Dusty. Dusty's family could afford things like mobile phones. He felt lucky to get new shoes once in a while.

Dusty and Curtis looked around the shop as they waited. It sold everything from bait to bread, eggs, and beer for the nearby rural residents.

Joe returned and handed the card back to Curtis, "I talked to Officer Corday. She said to stay put, and she would meet you here. Take a seat out front on the bench. Meantime, you can each take a drink out of the cooler on me while you wait. I'll get a bowl of water for Holler. It looks like you boys could use it." Joe walked away, shaking his head, wondering if the boys had really found a dead body.

The boys settled on the wooden bench in front of Joe's to wait for Officer Corday. They helped themselves to cold drinks from the cooler and watched a large shiny black Jeep pull in, and two men get out. The boys could tell the men were not local by how they dressed and looked around.

"Hey kids, a nice dog you have there. Bloodhound, right?" an Asian-looking man said. "You ever chase a man down with him?" he laughed.

"No, but he found a dead man in the park today. An FWC officer is coming to check it out," Curtis announced proudly, patting Holler's head.

That took the smile off the man's face.

"You don't say. Now that's interesting." Nodding to his companion, they walked into the bait shop.

The two men whispered to each other, looking back at the boys sitting on the bench. They quickly made a couple purchases and left the store.

The boys watched the men go, "Who were they?" Curtis asked.

"Never saw them before. Definitely not from around here."

Chapter Sixteen

Curtis stood up, smiling, as Liz pulled into the bait shop. Running up to the patrol truck, he stopped short when he saw an older woman sitting beside the officer.

"Hi Curtis, what's this I hear about Holler finding a dead body? Tell me about it," Liz said, stepping out of her vehicle.

While she talked, she ruffled Holler's ears. She glanced at her mother, pulling down the visor and checking her makeup in the mirror. *Always ready for a fashion show*, Liz thought, even in Zolfo Springs

"Dusty, me, and Holler were just messing around in the park. Holler likes to find stuff."

"Sometimes it's pretty disgusting stuff," Dusty added, making a face and holding his nose.

"We thought he found a dead squirrel or a raccoon or something, but it was a person. This guy was shot in the head, dead. It was creepy. Dusty and I figured we better call you to see what to do, being it was in the reserve and all."

"Yeah, we don't have cell phones, so we hightailed out of there and came here to Joe's and had him call you."

"Can you take me back to where you found the body?" Liz asked. At the same time, she wondered what to do with her mother.

"Did you talk to anyone else about what you found besides Joe?" Liz asked the boys.

"No, only Joe," Curtis said. He had forgotten about the Asian man and his friend.

"We'll have to go back to where you found the body right now. I'll call your parents and tell them you are with me. I'll take you home after."

Liz opened the back door to her truck, and the boys and Holler squeezed in.

Constance Corday wrinkled her nose and slowly turned her head to look at the passengers. "Is this necessary?"

"It's part of my job, Mom. I investigate things that happen in wildlife and state parks. The boys here have reported that they found a dead body, and it's up to me to look into it." Liz started the engine, pulled out, and headed for the entrance to the park.

Liz dreaded the day ahead. Dealing with a dead body was nothing compared to coping with her mother. She thought of calling Seth to help, but that presented another problem. How could she explain Seth to her mother without upsetting her mother or embarrassing Seth? Liz had planned on telling her mother about Seth but had not found the courage.

It was time. Liz took a deep breath and pulled out her phone. "Hi, Seth. Can you meet me at the entrance to the Zolfo Springs wildlife park? Remember those two boys from the other day? They say they found a dead body, and I could use another set of eyes on this one."

"Sure, I'll meet you there." Seth was over the moon that Liz had reached out to him, even if it was work-related.

"Eh…I have my mother with me for a ride-along."

"OK, fine. I'll see you in 20." Seth didn't know if that was a good thing, but he was about to meet Constance Corday whether he wanted to or not. The question was, did she want to meet him?

Having her daughter living with someone was one thing. Having that someone be a Seminole Indian was something else again.

Chapter Seventeen

Dusty and Curtis tried to scramble out almost before the vehicle stopped in the parking lot at the wildlife park. Liz had to unlock the doors for them first. The boys were ready to take off as Holler bounded away with the boys in hot pursuit.

"Boys, stay around here and don't go wandering off. You have to show me where you found the body," Liz shouted, trying to stop the headstrong young boys as they disappeared around the administration building.

"You can't be serious," Constance complained. "This is not a real job, trekking after two irrepressible urchins and a smelly old dog. I can't believe my daughter is trying to find a dead body in the middle of a…Oh, I don't know what this is." Constance stood beside the vehicle in her designer clothes and perfect makeup, clutching her Gucci handbag with a disgusted look on her face.

"Mom, you agreed to come along today and see what I do. You can sit on one of the benches in the shade or call an Uber to take you back to the condo. I don't care anymore."

Constance huffed and rolled her eyes, brushing imaginary debris off her blouse, "That's a great way to talk to your mother."

It was at that moment that Seth pulled in.

Liz watched a big sloppy grin spread over Seth's face when he saw her. She thought *that would not last long once he met my mother.*

"Aren't you going to introduce me to your co-worker?" Constance said.

Liz looked to the cloudless sky, said a silent prayer, and began. "Mom, this is Seth Grayson, my boyfriend. I live with him in Sarasota. We met working a poaching case a while back.." Liz had taken Seth's hand and leaned against his shoulder for courage. She could feel his body heat and strength even through his Kevlar safety vest.

"Please to meet you, Mrs. Corday. I hope you are enjoying your time with your daughter," Seth said, extending his hand.

"Eh, it's been interesting," Constance replied by only letting the tips of her fingers touch Seth's outstretched callused hand. She was studying Seth's face with questions rising in her mind, his eyes were grey-green and very captivating, and the parallel scar on his cheek made him seem mysterious. What kind of a man was this that my daughter had fallen for?

"We better get going. It's only going to be light for another couple hours or so," Liz said, breaking the awkward silence.

Chapter Eighteen

"Mrs. Corday, you can come with us if you want. The park has a lot to see beyond a dead body," Seth offered.

Liz was surprised when her mother agreed to join them. She had a funny feeling that her mother had an ulterior motive behind it.

The group followed Curtis, Dusty, and Holler deep into the park to the edge of the Peace River. Most of the way, they walked along a pine plank boardwalk. The walk was edged with saw palmetto, tall palms, and ancient oak trees. Small creeks and gullies running with rainwater supported the frogs and lizards on which the larger creatures fed. Snakes hid in the undergrowth, waiting for a meal to appear.

"How do you boys get in here?" Seth asked.

"We come in near my grandpa's place. My mom drops us off a couple times a week," Dusty said.

Pioneer Park was a favorite spot for day trippers, with hiking trails and a boat ramp. The park also had the Cracker Trail Museum and Wildlife Refuge. It would be a great place to explore for two boys and a dog.

"Yeah, we get the same deal that Lucy and Melinda get," Curtis added.

Alarm bells rang in Seth's head. He stopped walking and looked at the two boys. "What deal is that?"

"Well, the girls get one dollar for each little turtle they bring to my grandpa. Because we're older, we get two dollars each. Dusty and I came out here and along the Peace looking for turtles when Holler found the dead guy."

"We'll have a long talk about this turtle business of yours. Right now, we need to find this body."

"We're almost there. There's a mean alligator in this last creek, so watch out," Curtis said, jumping a log and hopping over the slow-moving creek. "She's got a nest down a ways that she's guarding."

Constance cringed at the mention of the alligator, grabbing her daughter's arm as she looked up and down the creek. Slipping on the edge of the creek, one of her expensive walking shoes filled with a murky sludge. Gaining her balance, Constance shook out her shoe and groaned, "This is so disgusting. How do you do this all the time?" she asked Liz.

"I love being out here, Mom."

"Just like your father," Constance grumbled.

"It's right up here," Curtis called, running after Holler. The dog beat them to the body, sniffing and pawing the ground.

"Call Holler back. He might mess up any evidence," Seth said.

"Come here, Holler," Curtis said. He latched onto the dog's collar and held him tight.

Dusty and Curtis stood with Constance as Seth and Liz examined the scene wearing latex gloves.

The body was a man in his mid-thirties, about six feet tall, well built, with a gaping bullet hole in the back of his head. He had been dead for at least twenty-four hours. The animals had been nibbling on the man's extremities. They were lucky the momma alligator had not made a meal of the body.

Liz checked his pockets for any identification.

"Nothing," Liz said, straightening up. "I'll call the Hardee County Sheriff and get a forensics team out here."

"Liz, take the boys and your mother back. I'll wait here for the forensics team. Once the medical examiner removes the body, I can join you. I want to talk to Dusty and Curtis before they return to their parents."

Seth watched them go and then began to circle the body. He saw three sets of footprints. Seth judged one set belonged to the victim. The other two sets were of different sizes. One pointed and smooth-soled. The other was a ridged hiking boot more suited to the terrain.

By the size of the hole in the victim's skull, Seth figured the gun used had to be a thirty-eight, maybe a Glock. The forensics would confirm that.

The shallow, amber-colored Peace River rolled slowly past where Seth stood. Turtles basked on moss-covered logs and half-submerged rocks near the edge. He noticed several places where tiny turtles had emerged from the sandy banks over the past few weeks. He only hoped they would make it to adulthood and replenish the species. Seth knew he had to find out who was trafficking turtles in his area and hope that this poor guy at his feet was not also one of their victims.

Hap Dunbar and his grandsons were involved with a dangerous trafficking organization that was willing to kill to keep its secrets.

Chapter Nineteen

On the way back, Dusty and Curtis helped Constance across the creek. Constance kept an eye out for the alligator they mentioned on the way in. It was late into the nesting season, and momma gators were very protective but not always sitting on the nest. Momma gator could be off hunting for her evening meal or watching from only a couple feet away.

Liz and the boys listened for the croaking of newly hatched baby gators but didn't hear anything. The only sounds were of the crows and scrub jays or the chatter of a squirrel scolding the intruders.

The forensics team pulled in as the group arrived at the park parking lot.

"They're coming now," Liz said, motioning to the forensic van pulling in.

Liz greeted Officer Perez, "Hello, I'm Officer Liz Corday. Officer Grayson is waiting with the body. You made good time."

"Yeah, Hi, Liz. Traffic was light for a change," the officer answered.

"Dusty and Curtis here found a body back in the park along the river. The boys can show you and your team the way."

Waving the boys up, Liz said, "Dusty, Curtis, you show them the way and come straight back here. Seth wants to talk to you about those turtles you've been catching for your grandpa."

Officer Perez's eyebrows rose, and he gave Liz a questioning look. "Heard that was going on in Lee County. Guess it's starting up here now?"

"Could be. We think our dead body might be involved but can't be sure," Liz answered. She radioed Seth that Officer Perez was on his way.

Constance sat on a park bench under an old water oak tree adorned with Spanish moss. Liz sat beside her mother and waited, watching the sheriff's team and a couple officers head out, following the boys and Holler.

Casting a sidelong glance at her mother, Liz saw the frown lines and the tight jaw. "Do you have something to say, Mom?"

"Yes, I do. Are you out of your tiny little mind? That boyfriend of yours is an Indian, a Seminole. I saw them at the Hard Rock Casino in Tampa," Constance said. "Think of your future. I can introduce you to some very well-connected professional men in Tallahassee."

Liz jumped up and faced her mother., "I can't believe you said that. You are unbelievable. Seth is a wonderfully caring, honest person. He loves me, and I love him. Maybe I want to marry Seth. I certainly don't want your country club lifestyle. I've told you that. You are a snob, and I don't blame Dad for leaving you."

Liz paced off a bit, fuming. She was also astonished at what she had just said.

"I'm only thinking of you." Constance fumbled in her purse for a tissue she didn't need. She was mad, furious that her daughter was not taking her advice. How could anyone prefer tramping around in the woods to fine dining and fashionable clothes.

Liz was glad she had finally dared to stand up to her mother and tell her about Seth. It was a relief to finally speak her mind and say what she wanted to say.

She was standing ramrod straight in front of her mother. She could inhale the Armani her mother bathed in, "I've met Seth's parents. They are warm and welcoming people. Too bad you couldn't do the same," she shouted and stomped off to lean against her truck to wait for Seth and the boys to return.

Chapter Twenty

"Officer Perez," Seth called, seeing the Hardee County sheriff's officer and the forensics team stumbling through the undergrowth towards him.

"Hello, Officer Grayson. I hear the boys here have found a dead body."

"Sorry to drag you way out here. Dusty and Curtis found the victim a few hours ago. It looks like the guy's been shot execution-style in the back of the head."

Perez knelt to examine the victim. He looked closely at the dried blood around the hole in the skull. "I think you are right. The bullet penetrating here." the officer indicated with a probe. "Exiting through his left eye in a downward trajectory. That would make the killer much taller, or our victim was kneeling when he was shot. He was shot at reasonably close range. There is gunshot residue around the wound and the victim's hair."

"That's pretty much what I thought. I've got to get the boys back home to their parents. Can you send me the report as soon as you have it? I have an idea it's linked to something I'm working on," Seth said.

"Will do, Officer Grayson. Maybe we can grab a beer, and you'll tell me about this case of yours," Perez responded. "I'd be glad to help if I can."

"Sounds good. Come on, boys. We've got to go." Seth had to pull the boys away from the forensics team. Curtis was especially interested in what the team was doing and all the tools of their trade. He was asking questions, and the men were engaged in helping him understand what they were doing. Seth thought that maybe Curtis had found a future career after all. He planned on talking to the youngster more about becoming an FWC officer. It was never too early to plant the idea of a promising future.

"Come on, Holler. We need to get back," Curtis said. Holler had his nose stuck in a palmetto bush chasing a lizard. It was dangerous for the curious dog to be doing as pygmy rattle snakes and the Eastern indigo, both very poisonous, liked to hide in the shade of the palmetto bushes.

"He'll follow along. I want to talk to you and Dusty about these turtles you have been collecting for your grandpa," Seth said while walking on the boardwalk toward the entrance to the wildlife park where Liz waited.

"We told you we get paid for every turtle we bring to our gramps. He has this guy that comes round and pays him for them." Dusty said.

"Did you ever see this man at your grandpa's place?" Seth asked.

"Nah, the man came when we were in school," Curtis said.

"How often does the man come around? Does your gramps tell you what size turtles to find?"

"Gramps said to get baby turtles, 'specially alligator snapping turtles, gopher tortoises, and cooters," Dusty said.

"Don't forget those soft-shelled ones. Gramps liked us to get those too." Curtis added.

"Yeah, that's right." Dusty agreed. "He gave us pictures of the ones he wanted us to look for."

"Boys, I hate to tell you, but what you were doing is against the law. Your gramps could go to jail if he were caught. All those turtles are on the endangered list. You need a special permit to collect them, and you definitely cannot sell them. I'll talk with your grandpa again and ask him a few more questions. Let's get you boys home. I'm sure your parents will be wondering what is going on."

"We didn't know we were doing anything wrong," Curtis said. The boy looked ready to cry. "We didn't know it was wrong. Grandpa said it was so we could make some extra money, that's all. Lucy and Melinda were finding turtles too."

Seth could understand how difficult it was for the young boys. They were having fun collecting turtles and making a few dollars and didn't know it was illegal. Even their grandpa didn't understand that it was unlawful, but the traffickers did. Hap Dunbar and his grandkids were victims in this.

Chapter Twenty-One

Liz checked her watch and figured Seth and the boys should be along any minute. She was leaning against her truck, kicking at the crushed shell in the parking lot, when she saw Seth and the boys coming down the path. It was hitting 90 degrees in the late spring sun, and she was boiling inside after the exchange with her mother.

Constance managed to get to Seth before Liz did, and Liz was not thrilled to see her mother and Seth talking. Considering their last conversation, she cringed inside to think what her mother might be saying to him.

Liz asked, "Hey, Chief, you find out anything useful?" She tried to sound cheerful.

"A couple things," Seth answered. "I had a long talk with Dusty and Curtis on the way back. They didn't' know what they were doing was illegal and thought it was just a bit of fun and a way to get some extra money."

"You talk to them about the turtles that Hap Dunbar had?" Liz asked.

"Yeah, and I have an idea our dead friend there by the river is involved. I have some thoughts to run by you.

"I've asked your mother to join us for supper at our place tonight. You can drive your mother back to your place after if that's OK with you? I want a chance to get to know each other better."

Liz looked at her mother, trying to gauge what she was up to again. "If it's OK with you, Mom. Sounds like a good idea."

"It might be nice to see where you spend so much of your time," Constance said. She tried to sound pleasant but missed the mark.

Liz did not have a good feeling about this. Her mother was unpredictable at best.

"I have to get going and take care of Nokosi. I'll get some dinner started and meet you there. Can you drop the boys off on your way to save time?"

Liz watched her mother roll her eyes at the thought of being stuck with the two boys and the dog again, but she was past caring what her mother thought. *Serves her right,* Liz thought as she piled everyone in. She turned her truck around and began the journey to deliver the boys to their parents and take her mother to Seth's place in Sarasota.

Liz spotted a black Jeep with its engine idling at the other end of the lot, behind a stand of live oaks and spiny palmettos. She was sure the men inside were watching them. Maybe they were just curious about all the police milling about, but then again?

Liz wanted to get the plate number but was distracted by Dusty. "Officer Grayson said he had to take care of Nokosi. What is a Nokosi?"

Liz watched in her rearview mirror as the Jeep pulled away.

"That's Officer Grayson's dog."

"That's neat. He has a dog like Holler," Curtis said.

"Yeah. Nokosi is a big dog like Holler," Liz said, cursing herself for getting distracted. *Oh well, probably just some noisy tourists.*

"Follow the kids and the lady FWC officer. I want to know where they go. It might come in handy if I need some leverage." Pham Pen told his driver.

Jarod Henderson did as Pen ordered him. After all, the man was paying well for his services. Henderson had been recruited to assist Pen with the trafficking operation but discovered that Pen was following orders from someone above him. Henderson didn't care for how Pen bossed him around and was uncomfortable with beating up an old man.

Chapter Twenty-Two

After dropping Dusty and Curtis off in Nocatee on the way to their place in Sarasota, Liz asked her mother, "Are you going to talk to me?"

Constance took a moment and finally broke her self-imposed silence. "So, tell me more about this man of yours. How serious are you two?" Constance asked, staring at the marshy roadside and wondered how her daughter could make such poor decisions in her career and personal life.

"We are taking it one day at a time," Liz answered.

"Then there is still time for you to change your mind and see reason, thank God."

"Mom, you just don't get it." Liz wanted to scream but held her temper in check. "Seth and I have no plans to get married in the near future. We enjoy our job and being together. That's enough for now. Maybe further down the line, things might change. But that is for us to decide, no one else."

"Ok, you like seeing dead bodies, catching bad guys, wearing a gun. You like being a wildlife cop." Constance was very sarcastic, and Liz experienced a flashback from her youth. How her mother would scold and belittle her father for wanting to go fishing instead of playing bridge with her Mom's stuffy country club friends.

"Look, when I met Seth, we worked on a case of alligator egg poaching." Liz saw her mother snicker.

"It was important. The poachers had allowed a young college

kid to get killed by an alligator. They were devastating the alligator population of Manatee and Sarasota Counties and selling the eggs illegally in Louisiana. Seth risked his life by going undercover at an alligator farm in Myakka to bring these guys to justice. He's one of the bravest and most honest men I know."

"Why does all this have to involve you?"

Liz put her directional signal on for the turn to SW Highway 72.

"Someone has to protect the environment and the wildlife for future generations, like these turtles and baby alligators. What these people are doing is stripping the species right out of existence. It's illegal. There are laws that protect the different species for a reason, and I'm going to enforce those laws." Liz was mad and didn't know how to get through to her mother.

"Mom, Seth told me these guys have already beaten an old man, Dusty's grandfather because he said he didn't want to collect turtles for them anymore. We suspect the dead man in the park had something to do with their operation. There could be more bodies if we don't stop them. What about Curtis and Dusty? Do you want them killed by these criminals?"

Constance huffed and stared out of the window.

Chapter Twenty-Three

Liz relaxed when she pulled in and parked beside Seth's truck. Nokosi recognized the sound of her engine and rushed out to meet her. Constance at first refused to get out of the SUV until Seth came out and restrained the oversized dog.

"Is that a dog?" Constance asked, raising her eyebrows and backing away.

"His name is Nokosi. It means *bear* in Seminole. He started small and cute and kept on growing," Seth laughed. "Come on in."

They followed Seth into the house, where Constance kept an eye on Nokosi while appraising where her daughter lived. The house was not what Constance had expected. It was neat and decorated with Seminole art, pottery, and handicrafts. The house had a calm and homey feel.

"Have a seat, Mom, would you like a cold drink?" Liz asked.

"Please," Constance said.

"I have supper almost ready. I wasn't sure when you would arrive, so I have some sliced ham, potato salad, and coleslaw. I have a nice white wine chilling and some iced tea," Seth said.

"Would you like tea or wine?" Liz asked her mother.

Constance took a seat at the kitchen table, still looking for Nokosi. The dog seemed to know his advances were not welcome and stayed at a distance. He stayed curled up in the corner of the kitchen, looking at the visitor.

"I could use the wine," Constance said.

Liz helped Seth set the table and told him about dropping off Dusty and Curtis.

"Their parents were displeased that the boys were brought home by the FWC again. They have banned Dusty and Curtis from visiting their grandfather and the park until further notice," Liz said.

"That's probably a good idea until we find out who is at the bottom of this turtle trafficking business."

Constance interrupted, "Tell me more about that. I don't understand why it's such a big deal. Surely there are plenty of turtles around."

Liz looked at Seth and let him take the lead. "Most people think the same way, but turtles are endangered in Florida and other states because of housing development, road construction, pollution, and environment changes. Man is a bigger threat to turtles than any natural predator."

Liz poured her mother more wine, "You've heard about human trafficking?"

Constance sipped her wine, gesturing with her glass for Liz to continue, "Yes, of course, I've heard of that."

"Trafficking in wildlife is also a big problem, but not many people know or care," Liz informed her. "Those boys we dropped off today. They were part of a trafficking ring and didn't even know it."

Constance looked thoughtful, "I can remember seeing turtles for sale in pet shops when you were little."

"It's all highly regulated now, from the size of the turtles to the species they are allowed to sell," Seth said, putting the serving dishes on the table. "Unfortunately, not all pet shops follow the rules. They are also sold online, which is another problem and even harder to control." Constance helped herself to very little from the delicious offerings. It was not what she was used to being served at her fancy restaurants or her snobby friends' homes.

After tasting a bit, she realized how hungry she was and how delicious the potato salad and ham tasted. It had been a long time since she had had a typical family meal. She wondered how long it had been and where she had lost contact with her only daughter. She tried to blame her husband for turning her daughter away from her, but it was after the divorce and Liz went to college that things changed drastically between them.

She slowly realized that her daughter was grown up, and as much as she wanted to control Liz's life, she couldn't.

Nokosi whimpering at the door intruded on her thoughts, and Constance realized Liz was talking to her.

"Sorry Liz, I was enjoying this supper very much. What's bothering your dog?"

"He probably hears a raccoon or squirrel he wants to chase," Seth said, getting up to let the dog out.

Nokosi barged past Seth and took off down the drive, barking and growling. They both watched a large black Jeep take off, kicking up dust.

"We've had a visitor. I've seen that same Jeep at the park," Liz said, standing behind Seth, her arms around his waist, her chin resting on his shoulder. "We need to revisit Hap Dunbar tomorrow. I'm sure he knows more than he's told us."

Chapter Twenty-Four

Liz took her mother back to Tampa and met up with Seth the following day west of Arcadia, ready to visit Hap Dunbar. Their patrols would take them in different directions later.

"How was your mother last night?" Seth asked. He hoped some of the tensions he sensed between mother and daughter had eased up some. "Did you have a chance to talk?"

"She was pretty quiet. I think she knows she can't manipulate me any longer like she tried to do when I was younger. I'm stronger now and know what's important to me."

Liz stepped up to Seth and hooked her fingers on his utility belt, pulling him close. "I'm happy now with my life, with you." She reached up, tilted his hat, and kissed his lips. "I missed you so much. Mom left for Tallahassee this morning, and I can't wait to get you all to myself tonight."

Seth held her shoulders, looked into her eyes, and smiled, "You read my mind. I can't wait, either. But in the meantime, let's see what Dunbar can tell us about this black Jeep."

Seth held the door open for Liz to climb into his FWC vehicle. She had to shove fast-food wrappers and other trash off the seat. "Ok, Chief, I see you have not been taking care of yourself the last couple of days."

"I kinda got used to having you across the table from me. It was lonely cooking and eating alone again," Seth confessed.

Bumping down the road, Liz asked, "What about Nokosi?"

"He doesn't like to cook." Seth laughed.

They didn't take long to reach the turn for Dunbar's place. His single-wide trailer sat at the end of the road. Dunbar lived near the end of a maze of dirt roads miles from where the pavement and most cell coverage ended. Armadillos, snakes, and occasional deer were more common than neighbors in these parts.

The children's paddling pool was not out front, and the place looked too quiet.

Seth pulled up in the drive and let the engine idle for a minute before turning it off. "It's too quiet. He usually has his grandkids here."

They got out and softly shut the truck doors. Seth motioned for Liz to look around the back while he walked up to the front door. They took the safety strap off their guns just in case.

The front door was unlocked. Seth opened it slowly and stepped inside, "Hap. Hap Dunbar, Officer Grayson, I'm here to check on you."

Drawing his handgun, Seth moved through the small mobile home. He was startled when Liz met him in a back bedroom.

"I found Hap," Liz said. "He's outback. There's a back door."

Seth followed Liz out to the rear of the trailer. Dunbar was floating on his back in one of two child-size pools. He was barely conscious. The bruises from his last beating were glowing yellow, blue, and black. Blood was leaking into the pool from a severe wound to the back of his skull.

"It's OK, Hap, we've got you," Liz told the old man, holding his hand. Seth dialed 911 and told the operator where to send help.

Liz tried to comfort the old man.

"Hap, can you tell me who did this?" Liz bent close to hear him.

The man was weak. There was no way of telling how long he had been out there.

"He came for the turtles. The bastard wanted fifty more. I didn't have many. The boys have not been able to help. The big one was going to beat me again. I ran out the back door and tripped over the pool, knocking myself out."

Dunbar tried to get up. He was getting agitated. "I have to save my grandkids. Pen is going after the boys."

"Save your strength," Liz said, pushing him back down.

"Hap, who is Pen? Is he the one buying your turtles?" Seth asked, leaning over Liz.

Dunbar nodded yes, struggling to stay conscious, eyes rolling. Nodding again, he whispered, "Pham Pen."

"Does he drive a big black Jeep?" Seth tried again to connect the pieces.

Liz rubbed Dunbar's sternum gently, bringing him back, trying to get him to open his eyes and answer Seth's question. "Come on, Hap. Did they drive a big black Jeep?"

Dunbar rolled his eyes in his head before he looked at Liz and nodded and whispered yes before he blacked out.

The siren sound of the ambulance echoed amid the oaks and pines.

Chapter Twenty-Five

Seth and Liz waited as the EMT medics attended to Dunbar and placed him in the ambulance.

Seth asked one of the medics about Dunbar's condition.

"He must have fallen pretty hard. He may have a fractured skull and a concussion. He'll need x-rays and further tests. His age is against him.

The sooner we get him back to the hospital, the better," the medic said. "We'll be taking him to DeSoto Memorial Medical Center. You can check on him later."

As the ambulance rushed away with the siren wailing, Liz turned to Seth. "Poor man, he was trying to make a few extra bucks the only way he knew how. Too bad it almost got him killed."

Walking back to their truck Seth said, "I feel bad for him too. He got mixed up in something he couldn't get out of. Unfortunately, he also got his grandchildren involved. But now we have a name, Pham Pen. Maybe Captain Jacobs has heard of him. I want to check on Curtis and Dusty. I wouldn't put it past these traffickers to make the boys pick up where their grandpa left off."

Liz and Seth were interrupted by a Hardee County Medical Examiner's office call as they drove down to Nocatee. Fingerprints gave them a name for the dead body in the park. He was Matt Troyer. A local man with arrests for robbery, assault, and drug charges. The record showed a sealed juvenile history stretching back to his early teens—a real piece of work who would do anything for money.

"Could be he was working for the traffickers and tried to take a little for himself and got caught," Seth said.

"Sound about right. It's another name for Captain Jacobs to add to the list. We have two names and a black Jeep that keeps turning up. After talking with Dusty and Curtis, I'd like to stop by the hospital before going home and check up on Dunbar," Liz said.

Chapter Twenty-Six

Curtis's mother was standing in the driveway when Seth and Liz arrived. Lorraine Dunbar was married to one of Hap's sons. She was a careworn woman who looked older than her twenty-eight years. She stood there dressed in her Winn-Dixie uniform, ready to head for her job as a cashier in Arcadia. Curtis's dad worked in construction. Long hours and hard work had him either out of the house or attached to the remote-control sipping beer. Lorraine Dunbar's work schedule left Curtis on his own for more hours than a young boy should.

"I'm so glad you're here. Two men came by and said that Hap had been hurt and wanted to see Curtis. They wanted Curtis to go with them, but I wouldn't allow it. I didn't know those men from Adam, and I wasn't about to let my son go off with two strange men. Even Holler had his hackles up, and he don't usually do that to anyone."

"Was it a black Jeep?" Seth asked.

"Yes, how did you know?" Lorraine asked.

"Mrs. Dunbar, where is Curtis now?" Liz asked, panicking that the traffickers had followed them and found out where Curtis and Dusty lived. They had to ensure that these guys did not get their evil hands on the boys. She didn't want to think about what might happen once the boys were no longer of use.

"I sent him to Dusty's house. My sister-in-law is Mary Beth Stirling. She's my husband's sister. I told him to stay there and not go with anyone, no matter what they said. Dusty has a bit more common sense than Curtis. I have to work Saturdays and figured it was the best place for him." Lorraine stopped to take a breath.

"I'm so afraid those boys have gotten into something nasty. Their grandfather skirted the law for years, and those boys listen to his tall tales."

"I'm sorry, Mrs. Dunbar. Those guys were right about one thing, Hap has been hurt and is going to DeSoto Memorial Hospital.

"Is there someone to watch the children if you want to go to the hospital?" Liz said.

"Mrs. Chavez next door watches them for me sometimes. I'll ask her."

"OK, we'll get an update on his condition for you. Then you can decide if you want to go or not." Seth told Mrs. Dunbar. "It might be a while before they know anything."

"I appreciate that. I worry about my dad and the things he gets into. He tries so hard to help me out. I don't know what I'd do without him."

Liz took the woman's work-worn hands in hers to reassure her that all would be well. "Don't worry. We'll check on Mr. Dunbar and the boys."

"Seth, we better stop at Dusty's house just to be sure the boys are OK," Liz said as she took off her hat and brushed a stray strand of her honey-colored hair back in place.

"I agree." Seth turned to Mrs. Dunbar, who was anxious to get to work.

"Sorry, officers, but I can't stay. I can't afford to lose my job." Lorraine said, fishing her car keys out of her purse. "Mrs. Chavez is with the girls today. She enjoys having them and spoils them with homemade treats."

"We understand. Just try to keep Curtis with you or at Dusty's for the time being. There's no telling what these guys are capable of."

"I will. But I have to be leaving." Lorraine got into her old Chevy sedan sand cranked the engine, rolling down the window to release some of the built-up heat. It had been sitting in the Florida sun for hours. While she waited for the less-than-efficient A/C to kick in, she called out, "I know you are trying to keep the boys safe. Thanks."

Lorraine's job at Winn-Dixie was the only thing that kept putting food on the table. The money her husband sent home never did seem to cover the bills. She couldn't figure out why.

Chapter Twenty-Seven

Seth and Liz drove the couple blocks over to Dusty's house. Holler was sleeping on the porch when they pulled in. Their tires crunching on the gravel woke him up, and he started to bay and bark, announcing their arrival.

"They have a great security system in place," Seth laughed.

"Too bad he can't carry a gun," Liz answered.

The cousins came bounding out the door to see what had set Holler off. "Oh, hi, officers." The boys looked very worried and confused.

Curtis came down the steps, but Dusty held back. Something was up if the officers were at his house checking on them.

"Hi there, Curtis. Your mom told us about the men who came to your house today. How are you doing?" Seth didn't want to alarm them.

Curtis sat down on the steps beside Holler, and Liz joined him. Dusty was more cautious, staying on the porch and leaning against the railing. This was more than just a friendly visit.

Liz took the lead with Curtis. "We have some news about your grandpa. He's been hurt again and is in the hospital."

"So those guys were not lying," Curtis said with a hitch in his voice, trying not to cry.

"No, they were not lying. But they were the ones responsible for his getting hurt. You would have been hurt too if you had gone with them."

Curtis let a tear escape and used his shirt sleeve to wipe his nose. Dusty kicked at one of the pickets on the porch so hard it cracked. "Those bastards. Curtis told me they tried to get him to go with them with a story about gramps being hurt and in the hospital. Officers, why are they hurting our grandpa?"

Seth sat down with Curtis and Liz. He didn't know how much the boys would understand, but he had to try.

"You know all those turtles you were bringing to your grandpa?"

"Yeah, he paid us for everyone," Curtis sniffed.

"We talked about this. It's against the law to take turtles from the wild—especially certain ones. If too many are taken, there are not enough left to keep the species going, and the turtles become endangered and eventually become extinct."

"Did my grandpa know what he was doing was wrong?" Dusty asked from behind them on the porch. He was still kicking away at the pickets but not breaking anymore.

"I think he did, but he didn't think it was that big a deal. There are a lot of rules to follow. Unfortunately, the people he was working with took a lot of turtles out of the wild. They sell the turtles for huge profits. It's called trafficking. It's highly illegal, and they will go to jail when we catch them. They will do everything they can to protect their profits and not get caught." Seth watched and waited for what he had told them to sink in.

"Thanks for telling us, officer. I guess Curtis and I are in danger because we know stuff," Dusty said, coming down the steps to face Seth and Liz. The boy was quick to see the danger they faced.

"Yes, I'm afraid so. You have to stay together or with your parents at all times until we arrest the men responsible for hurting your grandpa. You know what they look like now, so be careful. We will have to try and catch the turtle traffickers who did this and stop them from taking more turtles. It will take time."

Seth and Liz stood to leave. Dusty took his place beside his cousin, with Holler in between.

Curtis looked up, tears glistening in his eyes. "Officer Corday, you help people and animals. I'd like to have a job like yours someday."

"Curtis, you can do anything if you put your mind to it. I'm sure the FWC would love to have you. If you want, I can give you the list of what turtles you can and can't have and how many of each. Some of them you need permits to own."

"Gee, officer, I'd like that, thanks," Curtis said, color rising in his cheeks. "Officer, I don't read so good."

His cousin reached around Holler and shook Curtis. "I'll help you if that's what you want. I should have been helping you all this time. I'm sorry, Curtis."

"Thanks, Dusty. I'd like that."

Chapter Twenty-Eight

After speaking with the charge nurse, Seth and Liz found their way to Hap Dunbar's room in the hospital. The old poacher's head was bandaged, and he was hooked up to an IV fluid drip.

"OK, to come in?" Seth asked.

"Yeah, why not? You guys probably saved me from spending God knows how long out there. Maybe eternity. The skeeters would have eaten me alive when the sun started setting." Hap turned off the TV and pushed away the tray table containing the cold remains of a light meal and hospital staple of green Jell-O.

"Can you tell us what happed back at your place?" Liz said, pulling a chair up beside hap's bed. Her tone was soft and comforting, and she hoped to coax him to open up.

"Well, you know I was gathering turtles, and you have already pieced together that I was getting paid for it. After talking to you two, I decided to do the right thing for a change.

"Then this shiny new Jeep thing shows up at my door. Two guys get out, and one of them, a smart-dressed Asian guy, says his name is Pham Pen. He says he's responsible for the body in the woods, and the same thing could happen to me if I don't bring him more turtles."

Seth wrote the name down. "What did they do next?"

Hap looked at Seth, and a tear left the corner of Hap's eye. "They said, did I want anything to happen to my granddaughters or my grandsons? They were threatening my family." Hap stopped to wipe the moisture from his eyes.

Liz passed him a tissue from a box on his tray.

"I tried again to tell them that the FWC was snooping around, but this guy Pen just laughed, saying that he didn't care what the FWC did. I had a deal with him, and there were consequences for not honoring the agreement. I knew what he meant, and it scared the shit out of me.

"I bolted for the back door, tripped on something, and cracked my head. They thought I was dead and left."

"I'm so sorry, Mr. Dunbar," Liz said. "You're due to be released tomorrow, and we'll need a statement from you. One of us will come to your place, so you don't have to travel. We're checking on your family. Were glad to see you were not more seriously hurt."

Seth almost told the older man about the attempt to get Curtis and probably Dusty to go with them, but he didn't want to upset Dunbar any more than he already was.

Liz and Seth stood to leave when Hap stopped them. "I had my share of run-ins with you guys and spent a few days in jail here and there for poaching and breaking a few laws. But not this. I never wanted this." Hap turned his head away, staring out the window.

The nurse came to take Mr. Dunbar's temperature and blood pressure. "Looks like you can be leaving us in tomorrow. The doctor will be in late to talk with you."

"I can't say I've enjoyed being here, but everyone sure has been nice to me. I'll be happy to get back to my own place and some real food."

"We'll let your daughters know that you will be discharged tomorrow. You take care of yourself," Seth said, walking out the door.

Chapter Twenty-Nine

"You know Curtis is sweet on you," Seth smirked. "He wears this silly grin and goes all red the minute he sees you."

Liz threw the towel she was drying the dishes with at him. "He's only a kid."

"Yeah, a kid whose hormones are stirring."

"Very funny," Liz laughed.

Taking their coffee to the couch, Liz cuddled next to Seth. Nokosi was stretched out at their feet and snoring away. Liz was deep in thought. Could it be like this forever? She was looking to sell her condo in Tampa. What if it didn't work out forever? But then again, what if it did? Was she ready to take that chance? Liz didn't want to end up like her mother. She loved her life, her work, and Seth. At that moment, she almost made up her mind, almost.

"Hey, sweetheart, I've been researching this turtle trafficking." Seth reached over and grabbed a bunch of papers he had printed off the computer.

"Did you know that there are forty-nine licensed turtle farms in Florida?"

"I knew they had to have a license," Liz said. "But I didn't know there were that many."

"There are rules and regulations in place these places have to follow. They have to apply for the proper permits and cannot take turtles out of the wild for any reason. Most of these farms raise exotics from Asia for collectors and have even stricter rules to follow," Seth said, scanning the pages.

"A rule passed a couple of years ago banned the sale of wild-caught turtles," he said. "Some species, such as the imperiled alligator snapping turtles and Suwannee Cooters, are illegal to take from the wild or possess. And there are possession limits for other species such as box turtles and diamondback terrapins."

Liz sat up and took the pages from Seth. "These are the turtles you saw in the kids' pool?"

"I'm sure of it. I took pictures with my phone."

"I'm afraid the black Jeep has something to do with that dead guy the boys found. They watched us at the park, and I swear they followed us back here."

"That's the vehicle that tried to kidnap Curtis."

"Let's talk to Captain Jacobs in the morning. Maybe he can give us some more information on how this operation works. The turtles must be smuggled out of the state and then out of the country. It says the biggest market is in Asia. They have to be connected somehow. That's what we have to find. I'm also betting that's who killed our friend in the woods."

Chapter Thirty

Less than a week after Hap Dunbar was released from the hospital, Seth and his young officer in training for the day, Greg Jessup, were standing outside Loraine Dunbar's home with a Florida State Trooper. Loraine was sitting on the porch steps holding her daughters close. Tears running down their faces. Curtis slouched beside them, crying into Holler's soft fur.

Loraine looked up at Seth and asked, "Why would anyone do that to an old man? He never hurt anyone in his life. My dad was only out of the hospital for two days, and this happened. Who would do such a thing?"

"Mrs. Dunbar, I'm afraid he got himself mixed up with some pretty dangerous people. Did you have any idea that he was selling wild turtles?" Seth asked.

He felt terrible for the woman. Her husband was away more than he was home. She left her two young daughters with her father-in-law, Hap Dunbar, so she could go to her job at Winn-Dixie a few days a week.

"I knew he was selling turtles but didn't think much of it. He gave the kids a few dollars now and then for helping. I didn't know it was against the law or anything."

The state police were patiently waiting their turn to question Mrs. Dunbar. Seth stepped aside and sat down with Curtis and Holler.

"Mrs. Dunbar, I'm Officer Stevens, I know this is hard, but I must ask you these questions. You said you drove to your father-in-law's place at about 10 o'clock this morning."

"Yeah, I try to work when Curtis is in school. Lucy is three, and Melinda hasn't started kindergarten yet, so Hap watches them for me." She closed her eyes, and a new stream of tears escaped. "He used to watch them for me."

"What did you see when you got there?"

"The door was bust open. You know, hanging off the hinges, I had a bad feeling that something was wrong. I told the girls to stay in the car. Walking up the steps, I called out, but Hap didn't answer. I had to pull the door up off the floor to get in. I'm figuring he had a heart attack and stumbled to reach the phone or somethin'. He didn't eat right and never went to the doctor. Oh God, it was awful."

Deputy Perez from the Hardee County Sheriff's Department motioned for one of his officers to get Mrs. Dunbar a glass of water.

Having multiple police Agencies involved was stressful at the best of times. Flashing lights and patrol cars everywhere was not an everyday scene in this normally quiet town. Although crime was unusual, the town was growing, with the population reaching 30,000. The close proximity to Arcadia and Sarasota made it a good place for those jobs in those areas to raise their families.

"No problem, I'll get it," Seth offered, pushing up from his seat on the step and going to find the kitchen. He shook his head at the pile of dirty dishes and clutter. He had to wash a glass before he could get her the water.

Back outside, he handed it to Mrs. Dunbar, who thanked him before she could continue.

"Go on, Mrs. Dunbar," Officer Stevens said.

"Hap was laying there with this great big hole in his back. There was blood all over the place. Why did they have to kill him like that? He was an old man. He loved his grandkids and his family. Why?"

Officer Stevens hated part of his job, telling the family that their loved ones were not all that squeaky clean. It could wait until later when he had more information.

"Did you see anyone else on your way to your father-in-law's place this morning?"

"No, I don't think so. No, wait. A big black Jeep passed me, going in the other direction. I remember now. It was going so fast and almost didn't make it on the last curve. You have to slow down there or go off the road. Could that be the same one that tried to take Curtis the other day?"

Seth's head snapped at the mention of the black Jeep. Liz was right. That Black Jeep was involved. Now they had to figure out who was driving it.

Seth walked over to stand with FWC Officer Jessup. "It doesn't sound good, does it, Seth?" Jessup said. "Do you think it has something to do with that dead guy the kids found in the woods?"

"Officer Corday mentioned that she had seen a black Jeep the day we found that body," Seth answered. "She said it looked like they were watching what was going on. Liz put it down to just someone being curious. But then the same Jeep turned up at our place in Sarasota."

"That's a bit creepy," the young officer said.

"That Jeep is turning up in too many places to be just a coincidence," Seth said. "Let's check on Dusty. He might not know about his grandpa yet, and I don't want him hearing about it on the news or from some neighbor on the TV."

"What about getting someone to watch over Curtis and Dusty? Do you think the traffickers will come after them?"

"They might. I'll ask Perez to do a drive-by and keep a lookout for that Jeep."

Driving away from Loraine Dunbar's, he saw Curtis in the rear-view mirror. The young boy was still sitting on the porch steps. Curtis was wiping the tears from his face, still hugging his dog. He, most of all, was going to miss his grandpa.

<h1 align="center">Chapter Thirty-One</h1>

Seth was on patrol with his trainee, Officer Jessup, for the day, the radio started chatting, and the young man picked it up. It was a call about a fish kill at a large pond a short distance away.

"I'm tied up with this trafficking case. I'll have to pass you off to another officer to follow up on the fish kill." Seth said to the caller.

Seth arranged for Jessup to meet with another FWC officer to check it out.

"I'll drop you off, and you can meet Officer Harry Garcia. He's been on the FWC for about fifteen years and knows everything there is to know. He's a great guy, and you can learn a lot from him."

They could smell the dead fish before seeing them floating in the pond. Officer Garcia was leaning against his vehicle as they pulled up beside him.

"Don't you just love the smell of rotting fish?" Garcia said, trying not to breath too deeply

"Christ, Harry, this is a mess," Seth said, wrinkling his nose. "Yeah, the neighbors called it in," Garcia said, pushing his stocky frame up from the FWC vehicle. "It looks like some idiots let some hydrilla plants loose in the pond."

"Can I leave Greg here with you for a while? You heard about the death of Hap Dunbar this morning? It's now a murder case."

"Sure did. I arrested Hap a time or two myself. He was an OK guy, just always on the wrong side of the law. Heard he might have gotten mixed up with some turtle traffickers this time. Those guys are ruthless. They don't care about anything but the profits."

"Unfortunately, he also got his grandsons involved. It's a big mess. The traffickers have tried to kidnap the boys and may try again."

"What will we do about this fish kill and cleaning up the pond?" Greg asked Seth.

"I'll let Harry fill you in on that," Seth said. "The plant will have to be pulled out by hand, and then, unfortunately, some chemicals have to be added to the pond to kill the rest. It will take months to get rid of the hydrilla entirely.

"I'll have to go. I want to go back to Dunbar's place. I want to take a second look. I might see something the other officers might have missed." Seth wanted an extra pair of eyes and gave Liz a call. She agreed to meet him at Hap's trailer in thirty minutes.

Greg had wandered closer to the water's edge. "Hydrilla, that's this long green plant growing all over the pond?" the young officer said, pulling a branching strand three feet long from the pond. The plant was deep green with small leaves circling the stem like a bottle brush.

"Right," Garcia said. "It's a highly invasive non-native plant. It can grow six to eight inches a day. It depletes the oxygen in the water and leads to fish kills like this," Harry said.

"Where does it come from?"

"It's an aquarium plant, but some idiot just dumped it in the pond when they didn't want it anymore. It probably was taking over their fish tank."

They heard a loud splash on the opposite bank and watched an alligator chomping on a dead fish.

"At least the alligators will be feasting for a day or two," Garcia said. "The alligators breath air, so they don't feel the effects of low oxygen in the water."

"Hey, what's with them?" Greg asked, pointing to several soft-shell turtles slowly marching through the grass away from the pond.

"Those turtles are moving their home. The pond is no longer safe or able to provide food for them. There is a busy road out there in that direction. Let's gather them up and find a new place for them.

I think there is a good-sized pond in the new development down the road.?" Harry said.

They talked as they picked up the softshell turtles, putting them in the back of Harry's FWC pickup. They counted seven turtles to relocate.

The hard part was finding out who put the hydrilla in the pond in the first place.

Chapter Thirty-Two

Seth pulled up beside Liz in front of Hap Dunbar's trailer.

"Hope I didn't pull you away from anything important," Seth said.

"Not really. I was up on one of the boat launches along the Peace River, checking for registrations and fishing licenses. You would not believe how many people are ready to go out on the water without the right equipment."

"Oh yes, I would."

Liz looked at the ground kicking a stone with her boot. "I got a call from my mother this morning. She just will not give up. I told her I was selling the condo, and she went ballistic. My mother now wants me to rent it out just in case things don't work out between you and me. Can you believe that?"

"Knowing what you have told me about mother, yes, I can," Seth said, pulling Liz close. "She has no power over us. I love you, and you love me. Our future is up to us, not her." Seth tipped Liz's tan hat back and looked into her misty blue eyes before kissing her. "We will revisit this later tonight. I'll show you how much you mean to me and how much I love you."

"I love you too, my brave warrior," Liz said, kissing him back.

Stepping back, Seth said, "We still have a job to do. You ready?"

"Let's do this."

Instinctively unsnapping their holsters just in case, they walked up the rickety wooden stairs. The front door lay propped against the frame where the officers tore it off its broken hinges to gain entry. The door was in sad shape from whoever had broken in.

There was tape on the floor outlining the shape of Dunbar's body left by the forensic team. The blood was a sticky dark mess on the filthy tile floor, attracting hordes of buzzing flies.

Liz grimaced and shivered at the sight, waving flies away from her face.

"Come on. Let's see what else is here," Seth said.

Stepping around the gruesome evidence on the floor, they searched all the way to the back of the trailer, checking in the bedroom, only to find a mess of clothes, beer cans, and an old man smell.

The bathroom was disgusting and needed a good cleaning.

"I wonder if Lorraine Dunbar knows what conditions she was leaving her kids in? I don't think she came inside. Maybe she just dropped the kids off outside." Seth remembered the state of Lorraine Dunbar's kitchen. He might talk with Curtis about helping his mother out around the house more.

"Ah, shit, look at this," Liz said.

At the bottom of the bathtub were ten dead baby turtles. They had drowned in a couple inches of dirty brownish water with no way out. Several factors contributed to the death of these turtles. Turtles need to be able to leave the water to rest and regulate their body temperature—these poor things drowned in cold water with no way to escape.

Liz took pictures and made a note of the species they could identify. Each of the turtles was no more than three inches across, some as small as a fifty-cent piece.

"Do you think they were here when Dunbar's body was discovered?" Liz asked.

"They might have had a fighting chance if someone had found them sooner."

"Was Dunbar still collecting turtles?"

"If he was, why shoot him?"

Seth paused by the tape on the floor. "Dunbar was shot in the back, right?"

"Right," Liz said, wondering where Seth was going.

"He was running away from his attackers. I'm willing to bet the traffickers came back. They were threatening Dunbar again, and he made a run for it. The shot him in the back and killed him."

Liz and Seth returned to their truck, glad of the fresh air. The air in the trailer was stifling even with the A/C running full blast because of the open door. It smelled even worse.

Seth leaned over the top of his vehicle, waiting for Liz to get in and start her engine.

"I'll ask Officer Perez if they checked the bathroom and saw the baby turtles. We need to know if they were there and if they were alive or not. That might help to know if Dunbar was collecting again or not."

"I agree, Liz said. "Let me know as soon as you find out."

"Will do. I'm stopping by to see Curtis and Dusty before I head home. I call on my way."

"Good, see you later." Liz puckered a couple air kisses his way and threw the truck in reverse.

Seth sat in his truck with the engine running and the A/C high. The taste of death was still in his mouth. He called the Hardee County Sheriff's Department to reach officer Perez. Seth was disappointed and had to leave a message, but hoped for a return call soon. He had questions about the turtles in the bathtub that needed answers fast.

Chapter Thirty-Three

Pham Pen's enforcer, Jarod Henderson, watched the two FWC officers at Dunbar's place through binoculars from behind a large oak tree.

When they arrived at Hap Dunbar's last night, Dunbar had refused to open the door. Jarod was forced to break it down. The old man yelled that he was through getting turtles, telling them that the FWC was on to them, and bolted for the back door again. This time Dunbar hoped to escape and not end up in the hospital.

Pen ordered Jarod to stop him. Jarod shot, looking to wound the fleeing man, but Dunbar tripped, and the bullet hit lower, killing Hap Dunbar instantly and silencing him for good. It was Pen who came up with the idea of leaving a few turtles in the bathtub. He didn't care if they lived or died. If the authorities thought Dunbar was still collecting turtles from the wild, so much the better. It was a distraction.

Jarod waited until he saw both officers pull away before walking back to the dirt road and his vehicle. His phone rang as he turned on his engine.

"Yeah, they just left," Jarod said.

"Shut up and listen," Pen said.

"Ok, I'm listening."

"Our distributor is getting a shipment ready and needs turtles now. We are short one hundred turtles because of Troyer. We are shipping out of Miami and need to be ready by the end of the week.

The airport in Arcadia is expecting the package to be there for the trip to Miami. Everything is in place."

"How am I expected to get my hands on a hundred turtles? We just wasted a bunch back at Dunbar's place."

"I don't care how. Get on your hands and knees and find them yourself if you have to."

Jarod heard the click as Pen hung up.

Throwing the phone in the passenger seat, he growled and banged the steering wheel viciously with both hands.

Gritting his teeth, he balled his hands into fists, his nails biting into his flesh. Pen didn't fool around. Jarod had to figure this out, or he would be the body in the woods with a bullet in his brain. He also knew that a single hatchling could sell for over $16000 each with some species. There was big money there, and Pen wanted his share. Jarod just wanted to live. *Shit, I hate that man.*

He calmed down and pushed back in his seat. There had to be a way to get those turtles.

Those darn kids knew where to find the turtles. That was his answer. Get the kids to get the turtles. Problem solved.

Chapter Thirty-Four

Seth stopped by to check on Curtis on his way home. The young boy was still clutching his dog on the steps where he had left him. Dusty sat beside him.

The boys stood as the officer approached, "Hi, Officer Grayson. You catch who killed our grandpa yet?" Dusty asked, choking out the question.

"Not yet, but we have some ideas. Listen, boys." Seth had to make sure the boys knew how serious the situation was. "There are some pretty bad people out there. Your grandpa was dealing with men who trafficked turtles illegally. They killed him when he refused to help them anymore. Those men might come looking for you to help them find more turtles."

Curtis teared up, "Are they going to kill us too?"

"I'm not going to lie to you," Seth said, wishing he could tell them differently. "I want you to stay close to home. School is almost over for the year. Go to school and go home, nowhere else until we catch these guys. Do not talk to strangers. Call Officer Corday or me immediately if you see anyone cruising around in a black Jeep. Officer Perez will have a patrol car passing by, but you have to keep an eye out."

"Curtis, your mom could use your help right now. See what you can do for her and your sisters, OK? You know, pick up a little, wash a few dishes, things like that." Seth didn't want to come down too hard on the boy. Maybe he could figure it out on his own.

Dusty shook hands with Seth. "I'll take care of Curtis and keep an eye out. Thanks, Officer Grayson."

"Sorry about your grandfather. Call if you need me. I'll check back in a day or two."

Dusty and Curtis sat back on the steps to watch Seth drive away. They didn't see the Jeep parked behind an overgrown oleander bush at the end of the road. Jarod was watching.

"From now on, no more wondering in the wood with Holler," Dusty told Curtis.

"You hear that, Holler? No more wandering off." Curtis made a joke of talking into the dog's big floppy ear.

"I get it. I'm not stupid. Even though everyone thinks I am," Curtis cried.

He felt bad when everyone treated him like a dummy. He just had a problem with words. They got all jumbled up on the page. He did well when people said things instead of making him read.

"My mom left something for us to heat up," Dusty said. "You feed Holler, and I'll help your mum get supper ready. Then I'll help you with your homework. Only a couple more days of school. I'm staying over tonight."

Dusty realized that he would have to watch over his cousin and maybe grow up faster than he should because of what was happening. He could only hope he was up to the job.

Dusty's parents were not happy with what was going on and tried to talk him out of staying at Curtis's house while Lorraine was at work. The only way Curtis would stay at Dusty's house was if Holler could come too, and Dusty's mom was not going to have "that mangy mutt in her house."

The young boy realized something else. His cousin said he wanted to be an FWC office. What did he want to do with his life? He noticed the respect that the officers received and how they all tried to help his family. Maybe he might like to be a law enforcement officer. Dusty had to smile at that. His grandpa broke the law every chance he got, and now he was thinking of being a cop. Gramps would have a good laugh over that. Or think he was crazy.

Chapter Thirty-Five

Monday morning rolled around, and both boys were unusually happy to return to school. Staying home all weekend was boring. Even Holler seemed bored not being able to chase squirrels in the woods.

Curtis fed Holler and told him to stay close to the house. It was his mother's day off work, and she promised to look after his dog. Curtis was worried that if the bad guys came after him, they might grab Holler too. But Dusty told him that didn't make much sense because Holler didn't know how to collect turtles.

Before they knew it, the school bus was out front blowing its horn. Curtis grabbed his lunch and threw Dusty a paper bag with his lunch in it. They each had some change for milk in their pockets.

They were missing the few bucks they got from Hap. They raced out to the bus before it took off without them.

Pushing and shoving their way down the aisle, the boys went to the back of the bus avoiding the questions and stares from the other students. News had traveled fast in the small community about the murder of their grandfather.

Jimmy Henshaw, the high school bully, sat opposite them, throwing his big feet across the aisle. "Hear you two found a dead body? You got all kinds of police out your way, and I hear your grandpa was doing some illegal stuff that got him killed. Might a known it was something you trailer trash would be up to."

Before Dusty could stop him, Curtis threw himself at Jimmy

and hammered away at the older boy. It didn't matter that Jimmy was six inches taller and outweighed him by over fifty pounds.

"You can't say stuff like that about my grandpa," Curtis yelled, throwing punches at a startled Jimmy, who cowered in his seat. No one had ever dared to stand up to him before.

The driver quickly stopped the bus, grabbed Curtis, and marched him to the front of the bus.

"Young man, you behave, or you are walking the rest of the way to school," the driver said, secretly smiling. He was pleased that someone had finally stood up to that Henshaw kid. He debated reporting the incident to the principal or not.

The other kids yelled and cheered, slapping Curtis on the back as he passed them going down the aisle.

One of Jimmy's friends plopped beside the subdued bully, "How'd you let him wail on you like that?"

"Shut up," Jimmy growled. "I'll get even with that little cracker shit. He won't see me coming."

Dusty overheard the comment and was determined to watch out for his cousin.

No one noticed the Jeep following the school bus in all the commotion.

"I wonder why the bus stopped like that. No kids got on or off," Pen said. "We can't take them at their house or the school. There is a patrol watching the house. Maybe we can take them off the bus? I need to think about this. We need those damn turtles."

"What about all the other kids on the bus and the driver? I'm not sure that's a good idea," Jarod dared to say.

Chapter Thirty-Six

Seth stepped into the shower, surprising Liz, grabbing the soapy sponge loaded with her sweet-smelling jasmine shower gel. He rubbed it over her back as she lowered her head, arching her back, purring with delight. "You keep that up, and we'll be late for work again."

"We could always claim a flat tire," Seth said. Pulling her closer, he nuzzled her neck.

"I think we've had a few too many flat tires. That excuse is getting a bit thin." Liz turned to run her hands through his raven hair and playfully nipped his lips with her teeth.

Seth took her mouth with his and dived deep, taking her with him and enjoying the moment before they had to face the day.

"You know they already look at you funny when you smell like roses or jasmine in the morning," Liz laughed.

"They're just jealous," he said, inhaling the sweet fragrance from around her neck.

Liz said, "Ok, Chief, save it for tonight."

Toweling his hair dry while walking to their bedroom, Seth said, "I was thinking of calling my parents. We haven't been up to see them in a few weeks. There is a dance this coming weekend. We might make the trip up. What do you think?"

Liz thought a moment, "Yeah. I'd like that. It might help to take my mind off all that's been happening lately."

Seth pulled on his jeans and took his uniform shirt out of the closet. "I've been doing some reading online about animal trafficking. It's coming a close second to drug smuggling these days."

"I need coffee. I'll fix it while you let Nokosi out," Liz said, buttoning up her shirt and pinning her badge over her pocket.

After a quick cup and settling Nokosi for the day, Seth and Liz stepped out into a dull and dreary day of lingering fog.

"Yuck, I hate mornings like this," Liz moaned. The wet droplets hung in the air and clung to the Spanish moss hanging in the trees, making it sparkle in the early morning light.

"It will burn off fast once the sun gets up."

"I know." Liz opened the door to her vehicle and checked it out before entering. Ever since she found an enormous rattlesnake inside left by poachers intended to scare her off, she had gotten into the habit of checking.

Talking over the vehicle's roof, Liz asked, "What are your plans for the day?"

"I'm going to check out that honeybee farmer, Will Garrett, east of Arcadia, with that bear problem. The bear has torn up a couple of his hives.

We'll have to set up a live trap and try to relocate the freeloader to another area. Three Lakes Wildlife Area would be excellent for a young bear."

"I've heard of that place," Liz said. "It's near Kenansville, isn't it?"

"Right, It's the second-largest remaining dry prairie in the United States. At sixty-two thousand acres, it's all a bear could want.

Setting out the trap might be a good job for officers Garcia and Jessup. They can leave it overnight and wait for Mr. Garrett to call me when the bear is in the trap."

"You know who would enjoy doing that release with you? Curtis," Liz said.

"You're right. He would. It will depend on when we get the bear and if his mom lets him. I know he's thinking about the FWC when he finishes school. I also know he has some learning difficulties. Maybe we can help him out with some of that."

Seth gave Liz a hug and a swift kiss. "I've got to get on the road. I'll see you tonight. Stay safe."

"You too, Chief. Bring me back some honey."

"I will if the bear has left any for you."

Chapter Thirty-Seven

Liz hung up her phone shaking her head, concentrating on the road ahead. Her mother would not give up trying to run her life.

Constance Corday had come up with a new strategy. Since she couldn't convince Liz to move to Tallahassee, she would temporarily move down to Tampa and rent her daughter's condo until Liz saw sense and would move to Tallahassee and find a suitable husband.

Liz had argued repeatedly with her mother and had finally agreed to meet at the condo in Tampa later that day. Liz was seeing a real estate agent to estimate what she should ask if she decided to sell. Liz wanted all her options on the table before deciding what to do. She could rent it out but still have to pay the mortgage and insurance. Of course, the rent she got would pay for that but did Liz want that hassle? Throwing her mother into the mix was not helping.

Liz decided to check out Pioneer Park at Zolfo Springs on her way to Nocatee to check in with Curtis and Dusty. She could head up to Tampa from there on the back roads.

The park could get pretty busy on weekends, especially if an event occurred, like a craft fair or a car show. Nothing was scheduled, so today should be a quiet weekday, and she could park close to the boat ramp.

A young couple was unloading two kayaks from their SUV, and she stopped to lend them a hand.

"You have a great day for some fun on the river," Liz said,

As she approached the young couple. The early mist had risen off the river. The overhead trees dripped with Spanish moss like old men's beards, creating a cool green canopy. The slow-moving shallow Peace River was a retreat for those looking to get away and enjoy the sights of nature along its shadowy banks.

"I'm with the Florida Fish and Wildlife. Can I check if you have your life preservers with you?"

"Ah, I didn't think we needed them with a kayak. It's not a real boat," the young man said, frowning. "Besides, the river is not that deep."

The woman rolled her eyes, "I knew we needed them and threw them in the back. I'll get them," she said, walking back to their car.

"We rented the kayaks, and all the stuff came with them. We've never done this before. We're visiting my wife's folks. It's a bit too hot down here for me," the man supplied. "We came down from Michigan."

"You need to wear your life jackets. I know it's not deep, but the current can be pretty deceptive and is pretty fast in some places. And watch out for alligators," Liz cautioned.

Looking out over the calm, almost still water, the man turned a sickly pale, "Are you kidding, real alligators? I thought they were in the swamps."

Liz tried to hide a smile, "Any body of water in Florida could have an alligator in it, even backyard swimming pools sometimes. They'll do their best to stay out of your way."

His wife stood there holding the life jackets, chuckling, "I told you, Chris, about the alligators. The officer told you the same thing I told you. Now get in the kayak. We are going to have a good time. I promise."

"Are you planning on fishing today?" Liz asked, seeing a pole and bait in one of the kayaks.

"Yeah, I thought I'd drop a line to see what happens. I've never been fishing before." Chris said.

"I don't suppose you have a fishing license?" Liz asked.

Frowning again, Chris shook his head. "Never needed one.

I work for a brokerage firm in Grand Rapids. I've never fished in my life. Kayaking and fishing were all Laurie's dad's ideas."

"Well, you're not going to fish today either because you need a fishing license in the state of Florida."

"Spoilsport."

Laurie was listening and spoke up. "I'm glad because I don't want to catch anything and see it wiggling on the end of the line and trying to figure out how to get it off. I'm not the outdoor type as much as my dad wants me to be. I think he wanted a boy and got me. I'm happy taking pictures with my phone," Laurie added, slipping on her life jacket and handing one to Chris.

Liz watched Laurie put the fishing gear back in their car. Some cross words flew between the couple, but Liz hoped that the peace and quiet of the tranquil river would calm any hurt feelings.

Liz hung around to ensure they pushed off OK and waved as they paddled awkwardly downstream.

Glancing at her watch, she had just enough time to check on the boys and make it to Tampa to meet the real estate agent. She was not looking forward to a confrontation with her mother again.

Chapter Thirty-Eight

"Shit, there's that damn woman officer again," Jarod cursed, watching Liz pull up in front of the Dunbar house.

"We'll have to get those boys another day." Pham Pen said. "Sit here a minute. I want to see what she does. We'll have a big problem if she takes those boys into protective custody or moves them where we can't reach them." Pen and his henchman Jarod had been watching Curtis's house since noon, waiting for the boys to return home from school.

He needed to know their schedule to plan how to take them and make Curtis and Dusty get him the extra turtles he needed to make up the shipment due to leave in a couple of days. Pen thought about taking them off the bus, but too many things could go wrong with a bunch of kids and a bus driver. After thinking things over, he came up with the idea to grab them when they got off the bus before returning to Curtis's house. There was a small window of time before a patrol car would show up, courtesy of the Hardee County Sheriff's Department.

Seeing Liz ruined his plans for the day. They would have to try again tomorrow. Time was running out, and so was his patience.

Curtis saw Liz when the bus stopped and ran to greet her, a big lopsided grin on his face. Dusty was smiling but less enthusiastic. Dusty was troubled and more worried about things than Curtis. He knew the danger they were in was the reason Liz was checking on them.

"Hi, Officer Corday," Curtis said, color raising in his cheeks.

Liz remembered what Seth had said about Curtis having a crush on her and tried to keep it professional.

"I'm checking to see that you two and Holler are keeping OK. No strange vehicles cruising around?"

"We're fine. School's over in another week or so, and I can't wait."

"Can I get you a glass of cold tea, ma'am?" Dusty offered.

"No thanks, Dusty. I can't stay. Please, until we catch these men, stay close to home and out of the woods. These men are very dangerous."

Liz reached down to rub Holler behind his floppy ears. The dog closed his eyes and enjoyed the extra attention.

"Is your mom home, Curtis?"

"No, she had to work. Dusty is keeping me company. Mom said not to leave the house until she got home, but that's not until later." "Sorry, but it has to be this way for a while." Liz was worried that there was no adult with the boys, but Dusty seemed pretty levelheaded. If only the Stirlings let Curtis have Holler at their house, it would be much safer since Mrs. Stirling was home more during the day. "Holler ain't been out of the house in days," Curtis moaned. "He's bored being cooped up all the time. You gotta catch those guys fast so we can explore in the woods again."

"We're trying. Curtis, are you still interested in being an FWC officer when you finish school?"

"I sure am. I like the stuff you and Officer Grayson do."

"There's a lot of studying to do. You might need some help with your reading. I did some checking, and a retired teacher near here would like to help you. Her name is Nancy Taylor. I'll talk with your mother, and we can work out something.

"Dusty, you too. If you need help in any of your subjects. I'd like to see if you could do well and maybe attend college."

"Thanks, ma'am, I do pretty well in school, and my dad has a college fund set up for me. But Curtis could sure use the help, and his mom doesn't have money for college or things like that," Dusty said.

Curtis hung his head, and his eye filled with unshed tears. He knew he had trouble in school and wanted to do better. He hated feeling like the class dummy. Liz saw that he had never thought about college, but he did now. He had a goal.

"I'd like that, Officer Corday. I'd study hard if that lady could help me over the summer." Curtis said.

"There are scholarships for various reasons and for people who try hard enough. Let's see what we can do about catching these traffickers first—one step at a time."

Liz gave Holler another scratch and said her goodbyes, heading off to Tampa to meet with the real estate agent and her mother.

Pen and Jarod watched her leave and sped to the Arcadia airport to check the arrangements for their illegal turtle shipment to Miami.

Chapter Thirty-Nine

The Arcadia Municipal Airport was perfect for Pham Pen. He scanned the airstrips, one asphalt, one turf, and headed across the tarmac to the warehouses lining the opposite side of the runway tucked in behind the darkened terminal.

Pen had landed there from Miami with arrangements already made with contacts to get him started collecting turtles. Matt Troyer had been one of those contacts, and Jarod Henderson had been the other.

Pen had Jarod pull up beside the last warehouse in the row. It looked old and disused and perfect for its purpose. The name on the building had long since faded, and the color was now a mix of washed-out green and rust. The buildings were for storage and repair of the couple dozen planes based there. The airport had been a training field for WWII pilots and crew, one of a couple dozen fields during that era. The airbase was so busy in its heyday that it earned the nickname Aviation City for Arcadia. Today, the field saw three or four dozen private planes and a helicopter or two. Seclusion. Just what Pen was looking for.

Jarod opened the door into the dimly lit interior of the dank building. The interior smelled of rusted metal, rubber tires, and motor oil. Puddles of stale water sat on the stained concrete floor from holes in the roof. But something else hung in the fetid air, a swamp smell, out of place in the old hangar.

Pen walked quickly to a corner where a man was sorting silver dollar-sized turtles into plastic tubs on a folding table.

"How many have you got?" Pen asked as he approached.

"There are one hundred and twenty-three. I spoke with our man in Singapore. He has arranged an auction for the end of next week and is advertising that he has two hundred prime turtles. So, you can see we are a bit short of supplies. He has bidders looking for turtles for the exclusive pet trade and exotic food markets. Some of his more decerning clients are willing to pay thousands for the right turtle."

The man eyed Jarod and nodded, silently asking Pen who he was.

"Mr. Latimer, let me introduce you to my colleague, Jarod Henderson. He takes care of any little problems that might get in the way of our enterprise. My fixer if you will."

Jarod carefully disclosed the Glock in his shoulder holster. Latimer noted the foot-long Bowie hunting knife on Jarod's belt.

"Jarod, Maxwell Latimer is our exporter," Pen said.

"All well and good, Mr. Pen. We don't want to disappoint our contact in Singapore. He has a well-established network here who will hear about it and want retribution," Latimer said. The man was referring to an operation in Lee County that the FWC had shut down recently. Latimer knew a lot more than either man. The illegal trade of Florida's freshwater turtles provided millions of dollars in profits for international traffickers.

Jarod stood to the side, wondering about this well-spoken man who seemed to be doing the work of a flunky. Latimer appeared to be well-educated. How did Latimer know so much about the operation? Jarod thought Pen was the one calling the shots but maybe not.

Latimer reached into one of the pools and picked up a small turtle, "See this little fella here? He's worth a couple thousand dollars to the right buyer."

Pen looked at the turtle less than two inches across. "What's so special about that one?"

"This little money maker is a Barbour's Map turtle. You can just begin to see the spiny ridge developing along its carapace. They are prized as wedding gifts for the rich in Asian countries and can grow up to eleven inches across, larger if it's a female. This one's a real beauty, not many of these around. They are on the imperiled species list," Latimer chuckled as he returned it to the pool. "The rarer the turtle, the more it is worth. In Shanghai and Singapore, these little guys are worth a fortune."

In the corner in one of the larger pools, Pen heard scratching and clawing. "What's over there?"

"Ah, that's a special prize," Latimer said, beckoning them to follow him.

Inside the pool was an almost prehistoric-looking creature. "This is an alligator snapping turtle. He's still a youngster at seventy pounds and will keep growing and can reach two hundred pounds if he lives that long. However, I believe he will be some rich man's dinner long before that."

Jarod cringed, "You have got to be shitting me. Somebody's going to eat that ugly bastard?"

"Come with me," Latimer said, walking away from the pool to an area set aside for his office. He sat behind a metal utility desk and asked Pen and Jarod to sit in the folding chairs.

"Welcome to my office, such as it is. Let's get down to business," Latimer said as the door to the warehouse opened, and an attractive Chinese woman dressed all in black strode in. She was of medium height and thin, and her long black hair was braided and coiled around her head. Long metal hair pins held it in place. Pointed metal tips encased her fingernails.

"Ah, Meiling. We were about to discuss the finer points of our business. I'm so glad you joined us." Latimer's eyes did not show any pleasure at her appearance in the warehouse, even if his words did.

Latimer rose and bowed to the woman. Jarod thought the power had shifted again, and this Chinese woman might be pulling the strings. He was beginning to wonder who exactly he was working for.

Meiling perched on the edge of the desk, eyeing Pen and Jarod, "Who have we got here?" she said in slightly less-than-perfect English.

"Pham Pen and his colleague seem to have a problem with

their supply chain. I was about to talk to them about how we might rectify that."

"I don't want to know about their problems. I want to be able to deliver a product without delays. There are consequences for employees who cannot meet expectations," the woman said, playing with her long delicate fingernails. Jarod looked closer and realized that her nails were metal and probably sharp as razors.

Jarod swallowed and glanced at Pen, who had gone very pale. They already had killed two people for a few lousy turtles. Why was Pen so worried about this Chinese woman?

"We understand and will fulfill the order as expected and on time. You have my guarantee," Pen said. His life depended on it. Pen knew this woman by reputation, and that reputation was deadly.

Jarod shrugged his shoulders, looking at Pen, "What gives?"

"Later," Pen growled. He was beginning to stress and sweat.

Meiling took what looked like a long hairpin out of her hair and sliced through an apple sitting on Latimer's desk, laughing as she walked away.

Chapter Forty

God, this can't be happening, Liz thought as she pulled up in front of her Tampa condo building to see her mother's BMW parked beside the real estate agent's car. She was hoping to talk to the agent before her mother arrived.

Liz leaned back in her seat and called Seth. She needed to hear his voice and gain strength from him to confront her mother again. She was getting very tired of this battle of wills with her mother.

"Hi, Chief. Where are you?"

"On my way home from Arcadia."

"I'm at the condo. Mom is already here, and so is the realtor. I'm afraid of what she's been telling him."

"Sweetheart, take a deep breath and do what you think is best for you, not for her. Remember, I love you. Tonight, we'll have some wine. You'll tell me all about it, and I'll tell you about the bear that's messing with this guy's hives. Then a little more wine, and I'll show you how I can help you relax later in bed."

"Oh, I needed that so bad. I'm ready." Liz shut off the engine and marched into the building.

Liz was nervous riding up in the elevator. Could she stand up to her mother? She must be able to hold her ground.

Before the elevator doors opened, she hiked up her heavy utility belt. She decided that no matter what her mother said or the realtor offered, she was determined to sell the condo and make her life with

Seth for however long it lasted.

"Hello, Mom," Liz said, moaning as she walked in. Turning to the man sitting beside her mother, she extended her hand, saying, "You must be Mr. Richardson. Glad to meet you. Have you had a chance to look around?" Liz quickly changed to all business.

Mr. Richardson rose and presented Liz with his card. "I have been talking with your mother, and she indicated that you have decided to rent your condo instead of selling it."

"I'm so sorry for that misunderstanding," Liz said, glaring at her mother. "I am selling and as quickly as possible. I want to list it for a fair market value, getting enough to cover what I owe on the mortgage and some leftover for me to have."

Constance opened her mouth to protest, "Elizabeth, you can't do this. You don't know what you're doing."

A crazy thought of just pulling out her gun and shooting her mother to shut her up passed through Liz's mind.

Instead, Liz balled her fists, her nails biting into her palms. "Mother, I'm not going to discuss this with you. It's my decision. Sorry, but shut up or get out."

Richardson cringed at the exchange. "Maybe I should come back another time." He was extremely uncomfortable witnessing the interaction between the two women.

"Mr. Richardson, it's my condo, and I want to sell it. Please. Set the wheels in motion and send me any paperwork." Liz handed him her card with all her contact information. "Keep me informed."

Liz shut the door behind the agent. Turning to her mother, "How could you?" Liz shouted. "This is my place, not yours. I'm a grown woman and can make my own decisions. Whether you like it or not, I'm selling the condo and living with Seth. You can like it or lump it. I really don't care anymore."

Constance stopped, crossed her arms across her chest, and raised her chin, "If that's the way you want it. I was only looking out for your welfare. I don't understand how you can possibly enjoy tramping around in the woods, wearing a gun, and living with a man in a shack in the middle of nowhere."

Liz took off her utility belt, flinging it on the couch, and sat down, shaking her head. "That's the problem. You want me to live your life. I don't want your life. I want my life. That's why Dad left you. You wanted him to live the life you wanted, country clubs and expensive vacations to impress your friends. Everything was to impress others with how rich and wonderful you are. That was not Dad, and it's not me. Get over it. Go back to your country club and leave me alone."

Liz put her head in her hands and cried. She cried for the loss of her mother —a mother she never really had.

Constance didn't say anything. She quickly gathered her things and quietly closed the door behind her.

Chapter Forty-One

Liz fell into Seth's arms as soon as she walked in the door of their home on the edge of the Manasota State Park in Sarasota.

With tears running down her cheeks and her face against Seth's strong chest, Liz breathed out, "I did it. I told my mother I was selling the condo, and there was nothing she could do about it."

Seth held her, his chin resting on the top of her head, inhaling her fragrance. Letting her grieve for the mother she had just lost again.

"Sweetheart, I know how hard it must have been for you, but I'm so proud of you for doing what you wanted and not letting her bully you anymore."

Liz stood back and looked Seth straight in his gray-green eyes. "You know you're right. She was a bully. She bullied my dad right out of my life and tried to bully her way into mine."

She put her hands up and drew him to her, kissing him long, deep, and with all the passion she had in her soul."

Pulling away to catch her breath, Liz said, "I love you, Seth Grayson. You make me a better person because you let me be me. I love that, and you for helping me."

"I would never make you do anything you didn't want to do, ever."

Liz gave herself a mental shake and began taking off her heavy belt and uniform. "Enough of the soppy stuff." Liz wiped the last of the tears off her cheeks.

"I seem to remember there was something about wine mentioned, time to relax and talk about our day. Well, I've talked about mine. Without the benefit of the wine, I might mention, so how about that wine and we talk about your day and then do that relaxing thing. I could really use it."

"Happy to oblige," Seth said, pouring two glasses of Liz's favorite red wine. "You sit. I'll make up some omelets, ham, and cheese, OK with you?"

"Perfect, now tell me about your day," Liz said, sitting back and watching Seth at the stove. This was the life she wanted. A simple supper, a cozy home, and the man she loved were all she needed. Why could her mother not be happy for her?

Seth finished cooking and placed their simple supper on the table.

"Remember I had that call about the bear destroying beehives east of Arcadia? The owner of this small honey operation had tried everything he could to keep this bear away from his hives, and nothing was working. That's when he called us."

"I'm glad he didn't just shoot the bear. That would be terrible." Liz said. "The Bear Conservation Rule protects them. The only way you can shoot one is if your life is in danger."

"Right, and by the size of the tracks, this was a young bear. Maybe tossed out because his mother had cubs over the winter, and it was time for this young one to move on."

"It's too bad that we humans are taking away all the land that once belonged to the animals," Liz said. She was sipping her wine and rubbing her feet in Nokosi's soft fur as he stretched out on the floor in front of them.

"I looked around and walked into the woods in the back of Garret's place," Seth said, refilling Liz's glass. "It's pretty wild back there for several acres. There's open farmland beyond for a bear to wander in unseen. I hate to see the animals displaced, but there is no easy answer."

Nokosi turned his giant head, looked up at Liz with soulful eyes, and whined for his supper. "Oh, poor baby, did you think we forgot about you?" Liz fixed Nokosi's bowl while Seth washed the dishes.

Taking the last of the bottle of wine and two glasses to the couch, Liz asked, "So the plan for this bear is still for trying to trap and release him somewhere?"

"That's the plan. I'm having Officer Garcia deliver the trap to the honey farm. I want to take another ride out there in the morning, but with everything else going on, I want to stay close."

"Garcia will have some ideas on where to place the trap when he delivers it, and he will have Jessup with him. They seem to be making a good team."

Seth picked up the empty glasses, rinsed them out, and set them on the side. He leaned back against the counter, "I thought we could take a trip to Three Lakes Park to release him and stop at my parent's place on the way back."

Liz entered the kitchen, stretching her arms around Seth and laying her head on his chest, hearing his heartbeat.

"I'd like that." Liz was quiet for a moment. "I know we talked about taking Curtis to see the bear released, but that might mess up seeing your parents on the way back."

"You are the most wonderful, thoughtful person I know." Seth leaned over and kissed Liz. "Curtis is sweet on you, and if he were a few years older, I'd be jealous as hell. But I'm going to call my parents and see if they'd mind an extra visitor. Curtis was asking about me being a Seminole. Let's show him some Seminoles."

"Oh, he would love that. I can't wait to tell him.

Chapter Forty-Two

Pen and Jarod sat with the A/C going while they waited for the bus to bring Curtis and Dusty back from school.

Pen rechecked his watch. The time didn't seem to be moving since the last time he checked it. He was nervous that the patrol car would arrive before the school bus, and they would miss their chance at grabbing the kids and their only shot at getting the turtles they needed.

"What's up with you and the Chinese chick?" Jarod hesitated to ask, but he had to know where he stood. "I thought you were running this operation."

"Her father is a very influential businessman in Singapore. He runs an import and export business, not all of it legal. There are rumors that he is the head of a powerful criminal enterprise in mainland China." Pen didn't have the patience to try and explain to Jarod what a Chinese Triad organization was or that it could even be more dangerous than the Mafia.

Jarod was a country boy with a tenth-grade education and liked busting heads and scaring people. What he didn't like was not knowing what he was getting into.

"What's that got to do with the woman?"

"I don't pay you to ask questions," Pen said. "A criminal enterprise is like a gang but more organized. They are sophisticated and ruthless, corrupting the police and other officials to do what they please. Meiling Yang is a henchman for her father. She is highly trained and likes to kill for fun."

"Shit," Jarod mumbled, sinking back into his seat.

Pen poked him in the ribs to get his attention. The school bus was coming. "Pay attention and watch for the patrol car. We only have a few minutes."

Pen had Jarod pull up behind where the bus stopped, lights flashing to let a half-dozen kids off. On the quiet street, no other traffic was around. The middle-grade kids waved their goodbyes, scattering in different directions and leaving Dusty and Curtis alone.

The Jeep crawled on as the bus drove away. They slowly followed the boys to their front door, where they stopped and got quietly out.

Holler bounded off the porch and greeted the boys with sloppy kisses and rough play.

"Hey, boy, did you miss me? Only a few more days, and we're free for the summer," Curtis said, wrapping his arms around the big hound.

Holler's ears perked up, and Curtis felt a growl rumble deep in his dog's chest. "What the matter, boy?" Curtis looked around. He expected a snake. Instead, he saw a man reaching for him. The man was huge in the young boy's eyes and muscled, his arms covered in tattoos and scary as all get out.

Curtis saw another shorter man with a knife close to Dusty's side. They were the same men they had seen at the bait shop.

Holler broke away from Curtis and charged. Jarod's size fourteen boot caught the animal in the side, sending him yelping and whining onto the grass.

"You bastard. You hurt my dog. I'll get you for that," Curtis yelled. He aimed a kick that glanced off Jarod's shin.

Jarod snickered at the boy's feeble attempts. He picked Curtis up over his shoulder and carried him to the Jeep, throwing him in the back seat. With a knife to his ribs, Dusty had no choice but to get in with his cousin.

Curtis was struggling to open the locked door. "Let me out, let me out." He shouted. "You hurt my dog."

"Shut up and sit still. You're going to help us find some turtles," Pen shouted. He was secretly proud that he had a way to fulfill his contract and maybe save his life.

As the truck sped away, Curtis looked back, tears racing down his face, seeing Holler trying to get up and baying for help.

Chapter Forty-Three

When Seth and Liz arrived, the rural road was alive with law enforcement vehicles. Desoto County sheriff's cars lined the street. The small rural town of Nocatee, a few miles southwest of Arcadia, was not used to this kind of activity.

Lorraine Dunbar was sitting on the porch steps with an older woman. Seeing the officers pull up, she ran to them, shouting, "You promised to keep them safe. Someone took the boys. They almost killed Holler. How could you let this happen?"

Seth met up with Dusty's parents, Mr. and Mrs. Stirling, and took them off to the side so Liz could deal with Lorraine. They would get all the parents together soon.

Liz took Lorraine by the arm and gently led the woman back to the porch. "I'm so sorry. These men took advantage of a gap in protective coverage. Did you see what happened?"

The woman sitting beside Lorraine interrupted, "I did. I saw the whole thing. Lorraine was at work, but she told me what was happening with everyone. I used to babysit sometimes and all the time now that Hap is dead. I was watching out for the boys to come home from school."

Liz waited patiently. "Can I have your name, ma'am?"

"Oh, sorry, Mrs. Chavez. I live next door."

"Thanks, please go on," Liz said to the older Hispanic woman.

"Curtis and Dusty like my cooking. The girls like to help me bake. Lorraine doesn't have time for much because of working and all." Mrs. Chavez patted Lorraine on the arm, "Sorry, dear, it's not your fault."

Looking back at Liz, Mrs. Chavez said, "I don't mind cooking. I no longer have anyone to do it for; it helps pass the time. I like having the children around."

"Ok, the boys got off the bus. Then what?" Liz asked, steering Mrs. Chavez back on track.

"I saw the boys get off the bus and was going to call them to get some empanadas when this black SUV thing stopped in front. Quick as a rabbit, these two thugs get out and drag Curtis and Dusty into the thing."

"Can you describe the men?"

"One was short, like me, about five foot five. The other was over six feet. My husband was six-foot-two, and this man was taller and built like a wrestler or one of those football players with no neck. He had lots of those tattoos on his arms,"

Mrs. Chavez put her arms around Lorraine., "But poor old Holler, he tried to help, but that big brut of a man kicked him so hard I thought he'd killed him. The dog was whining and crying, trying to get up. First, I called the sheriff, and then I called my son, Richie. He knows a vet, and he took Holler there straight away. He called from the vet's office, and Holler has a cracked rib and some bad bruising, but he should be OK. The vet is keeping Holler overnight to be on the safe side."

"What about the boys? Do you know who took them?" Lorraine looked up through red-rimmed eyes.

"We have an idea. We'll do everything we can to return the boys safely soon."

"Oh, would this help? I took a picture of their license plate with my phone when they drove away. I always carry it in my pocket."

Liz shouted, "Seth, come here quick. Mrs. Chavez took a picture of the Jeep's license plate that took the boys."

"Mrs. Chavez, I could kiss you." Seth leaned over and kissed the older woman on the cheek, watching her wrinkled cheeks blush.

Chapter Forty-Four

Dusty tried to comfort his cousin, but Curtis kept crying and shouting. "You hurt my dog. I'll get you for that."

"Shut that damn kid up," Pen yelled. "I'm trying to drive."

Jarod turned in his seat, pointing his gun at the boys in the back. "You heard the man. Now shut the fuck up. We're tired of listening to you."

The SUV pulled to a stop in a secluded area at the back of Pioneer Park in Zolfo Springs, not far from the junction of SR 64 and SR 17. The park was an hour east of Sarasota and felt like a step back in time to the Florida of old before the developers and Disney.

They waited in the vehicle while a young couple packed their kayaks and left the Peace River boat ramp. It was late afternoon now, and the park was deserted.

"Get out," Pen roughly ordered. Jarod reached in and grabbed Dusty, pulling him out and tossing him to the ground. Curtis put up a fight, kicking and hitting and mostly not connecting. He stopped when Pen put a handgun to Dusty's head, "I only need one of you to find turtles for us. Two will get the job done faster."

Curtis wiped his face on his sleeve and slowly climbed out of the vehicle. His eyes never left the gun trained on his cousin's head.

"You take that one," Pen said to Jarod, nodding at Dusty. "I'll take the crybaby here." Pen grabbed Curtis's left arm, squeezing harder than he needed to. Curtis winced in pain and struggled not to cry out.

Turning to the boys, Pen said, "You are going to get us some turtles. My friend here will take one of you, and I'll take the other to cover more ground. I don't care if we have to stay out here all night. Either of you tries to run, and the other one dies. You understand what I'm saying?"

"Yes, sir," Dusty mumbled.

"You understand," Pen shouted at Curtis, shaking him.

Dusty silently mouthed the word to say yes, and Curtis whispered, "Yes."

Pen shook him again, "I can't hear you."

"Yes, sir, I understand," Curtis cried.

"Let's go. I don't want to be out here any longer than necessary."

Pen opened the back of the Jeep, handed Jarod a bucket, and took one for himself

Jarod and Dusty walked west, keeping the sandy banks of Peace River in sight.

Dusty stopped and pointed, "There." Several red-bellied turtles were basking on a log half submerged in the sandy bank. Dusty crept, but the older, wiser adults dropped into the swift-moving water. He grabbed up five little ones, about two inches across, and dropped them in the bucket.

"That's a good start," Jarod said, clapping Dusty on the back while giving him a shove. "Keep going."

Walking along the river, Dusty found a few more, but time was running out.

Dusty led Jarod to the shores of Twin Lake. The sun was beginning to set, and the moon had not yet risen. A movement in the grass beside the river caught Dusty's attention. Creeping slowly, he bent down and came up with a striped mud turtle. He circled the lake and found five more, all juveniles.

Slapping at mosquitoes, Jarod said, "Let's go back and see what your friend found."

Walking back, Dusty figured he had nothing to lose by asking a few questions. "Why are you doing this?"

"For the money, stupid," Jarod said, giving Dusty a shove.

"But why kill my grandpa? He was just an old man."

"My boss needs turtles, and your grandpa decided not to cooperate. He knew too much about us. Pen told me to fire a warning shot at him to keep quiet. I wasn't trying to kill him. He ran and tripped as I fired."

"So, I'm thinking that Curtis and I also know too much and will have to be silenced?" Dusty was afraid of the answer to that question.

"Look, kid, it's not my call."

Dusty could only hope that Curtis was behaving and not giving that other guy any reason to hurt him. He was relieved to see Curtis standing at the rear of the Jeep, loading a bucket into the vehicle.

With a big grin, Curtis ran to his cousin and hugged him. "I was so afraid I would never see you again." Looking over his shoulder, he whispered to Dusty, "That guy Pen is a cruel bastard." Dusty examined a bruise on his cousin's cheek near his left eye.

"He hit you?"

"Yeah, once when I argued about going in the water, he kept shoving me and making me go after soft shell turtles where I knew there were alligators. I found three snapping turtles but not the alligator snapping turtles he wants."

"I haven't seen alligator snapping turtles in a while," Dusty said, thinking back to what Officers Grayson and Corday had said about endangered turtles.

"That Pen guy didn't care if I got hurt or killed so long as I found turtles for him." Curtis continued. "I got him some mud turtles from around Rock Lake. I found some box turtles on the way back. He wouldn't even help carry the bucket. Dusty, I'm scared and want to go home." A tear escaped running down the young boy's face. "I want to know if Holler is OK."

Chapter Forty-Five

Seth paced in front of Lorraine Dunbar's house while Liz sat inside with the boys' parents. Mrs. Chavez was making coffee for everyone.

Mr. Stirling suddenly stood up, asking, "What are you doing to find my son?" He was getting agitated and not helping the situation. "I knew getting involved with that side of the family was a bad idea."

Mrs. Stirling sat quietly, holding a shaking coffee cup. "They're cousins," she said in a stage whisper to her husband. "Are you going to ban them from seeing each other? They go to school together and have the same friends."

"Maybe they wouldn't be in this mess if I had."

Mary Beth Stirling stood up, hands on hips, ready to fight, "You never liked my family. My brother works hard for his family. So, he doesn't work in an office like you, but tries his best. Mike, you were lucky, had an excellent education, and went to college. Some of us were lucky to finish high school and get jobs."

"So, it's my fault I got a good education and have a good job?" Bob Stirling stood up and looked out the window before turning back to his wife.

"I didn't say that. My father did all he could for my brother and me after mom died. I never thought of you as a snob, Mike Stirling, but you are a damn snob." Mary Beth shouted the last at her husband.

That brought Mike up sharp, "You're right. I do…did look down on your father for all the trouble with the law he got into and the way he lived." Mike turned his back, and his shoulders sagged. Returning, he reached out to his wife. "I'm sorry. I don't always realize what others have to go through in life."

Seth's mobile phone rang. "It's Captain Jacobs."

The room went silent, waiting for news on the men who took the boys or if anyone had found them.

"Right, thanks," Seth said, hanging up. "The Jeep SUV is a rental. They traced it to a rental agency in Arcadia. Captain Jacobs tried calling, and they are closed for the night."

"I guess we're going to Arcadia tomorrow morning," Liz said.

"I want to be there when they open the doors."

Seth and Liz drove home to Sarasota after leaving contact numbers with the families.

Lorraine told them that she had contacted her husband, Bob Dunbar, and he was on his way home from a job site in Gainesville. Lorraine silently cursed her husband for not coming home when she told him his father had been killed. His excuse was that he needed the work to make money to bury the old man. Hap Dunbar's funeral was on hold for the moment.

Lorraine didn't totally believe it. Her husband was staying away more and more as time went on. She was beginning to wonder if he had found someone else. The money he sent home was not enough to take care of the family.

Mrs. Chavez offered to stay with Lorraine and help care for the little ones. Lorraine was a mess, worn out from work and worried about Curtis, her father-in-law, being murdered and taking care of it all on her own.

Mrs. Chavez was afraid the young mother was headed for a breakdown if she didn't get some help.

Lorraine watched her sister-in-law and her husband get into their shiny late-model Ford, seeing the taillights fade down the country road.

She envied Mary Beth and how she managed to snag Mike Stirling. When they met, Mary Beth worked in a 7-Eleven, and Mike was a bank manager. He'd come in for coffee. She started giving him a free cup now and then. It wasn't long before she was pregnant with Dusty.

Lorraine was young and foolish and fell for Mary Beth's brother, Bob Dunbar, and his rugged charms. Within a couple months of dating, she was pregnant with Curtis.

The only difference was that Mike was a bank manager with a future, and Bob was a manual laborer with no education. Looking back, she realized how stupid she had been.

Now, thanks to Hap Dunbar and his lawless ways, both families may lose a child.

Chapter Forty-Six

Seth woke up to find a wet nose in his face. "Hey there, you need to go out and chase some squirrels?"

Rolling over, Seth checked the time and poked Liz to wake her. "Come on, sleepy head, we need to get a move on if we want to be in Arcadia when the car rental place opens."

"Oh, do I have to?" Liz groaned, pulling the covers over her head.

"Yes, you do. I need your company and your brain on this."

Liz groaned again, throwing the covers off, and grudgingly climbed out of bed. "I'll toss you to see who makes coffee?"

"I'll make the coffee if you put Nokosi out. We can both get dressed while he does his thing,and the coffee is doing its thing."

Liz walked up behind Seth, threw her arms around him, and buzzed his neck. "I love the way you think. Come on, Nokosi. Maybe you can actually catch one of those pesky squirrels today."

Coffee in travel mugs and Nokosi settled for the day. Seth and Liz left and hit the road for Arcadia.

"I'm so worried about Curtis and Dusty and what these traffickers might do once they don't need them anymore," Liz said. She watched the GPS screen for their destination. Sometimes the signal died out there in the sticks.

"I only hope we catch them before they get to that point. The traffickers have to ship the turtles out of the country. There are two main ports, Orlando and Miami," Seth said. "I did some research, and Miami seems to be the main distribution point for this kind of trafficking."

"In your research, did it say how they ship the turtles? You can't just put them in a box labeled *live turtles*."

Seth called U.S. Customs and Border Inspection to find answers. He was astounded by the different ways traffickers and smugglers used to move animals illegally in and out of the country.

"It took finding the right person. Officer Ellis works at Miami International. He explained how they check the cargo, and anything suspicious is x-rayed. Suspect packages are opened and taken apart to find any contraband and illegal items. US Customs and Border Inspection Officers check packages entering and leaving the country. If they suspect anything animal-related, they call in the Florida Fish and Wildlife Commission. That's us."

"There is also airport security watching for suspicious passengers who might have anything illegal in the passenger terminal."

"I bet he has some stories to tell."

"He told me one story about this man coming in from South America with baby parrots stuffed in the crotch of his pants."

"You've got to be kidding," Liz laughed.

"Seriously, I could listen to him for hours, but I only had a few minutes and was only interested in how to transport turtles and keep them alive."

Liz looked at the GPS again, "We're almost there. What did Ellis say?"

"He said they don't need to be kept in water. They could drown in water. The turtles only need to be kept damp. Some of them will die, but most make it."

"The poor things. All this to end up as someone's pet."

"Or worse. Someone's dinner."

"Sorry, I can't imagine eating a turtle. I heard people do, but not me."

"It was on the menu a lot for the old Cracker Floridians. I asked my mom about it. Turtles were a regular part of the diet back decades ago."

"Ew, yuck," Liz said, grimacing. She pointed to the car rental sign on the left. Seth waited for cars to pass before pulling into the lot.

A young man in a company tee shirt unlocked the front door just as they were parking. "'Morning officers, what can I do for you? Do you need a rental?" The young twenty-something was off balance seeing two FWC officers first thing in the morning.

"I'm Officer Grayson, and my partner is Officer Corday. We need to check who rented a black 2022 Jeep Grand Cherokee a few days ago."

"I'm not sure I'm supposed to give out that information on our customers," the man said, panicking.

Liz read the name on his pocket, "Eh, Jeff," putting a hand on her gun, "this is a double murder investigation, and two young boys have been kidnapped possibly by the men who rented that Jeep. Officer Grayson and I are law enforcement, and we will see that record, or I will arrest you for obstruction. Now may we see that record?"

Jeff nodded, "Yes, yes, right this way. No problem." He dug furiously in a file cabinet, pulled out the rental agreement, and handed it to Liz. His hands were shaking nervously.

Seth and Liz looked it over and saw the name of the person renting the vehicle.

"It says here, Matt Troyer," Seth looked at Liz.

"He's our dead guy in the park," Liz said.

"Did you say, dead guy? The guy who rented the Jeep is dead?" Jeff was definitely panicking now, wondering how he would get his vehicle back and if the insurance would cover any damage.

"Jeff, was anyone else with Mr. Troyer when he came in to rent the vehicle?" Seth said.

"Yeah, this creepy little Chinese guy and another man must have been over six feet. The Chinese one seemed to be running things." Jeff was relaxing now that he was helping and could answer questions. Maybe his boss might not fire him after all.

"By any chance, do you have CCTV?" Liz said, mentally crossing her fingers. Video could be a real break if they could see who they were dealing with and identify them.

"Oh wow, we do. Sometimes the customers get upset when we find scratches, claiming it wasn't their fault. The manager has the videos in his office. I'll set it up for you."

"We only need the tape for the date on the rental agreement. It says here the vehicle is due back Saturday. Today is Thursday," Seth said, looking at the agreement.

"Liz, we don't have much time to find the boys. I'm calling Captain Jacobs to fill him in on what we have so far. Can you look at the tape and see if you can spot Matt Troyer and the other two? If we send it to the captain, maybe he can positively identify them."

Pulling Liz aside, Seth spoke softly, "They don't intend to return the vehicle. They'll dump it and probably torch it to destroy fingerprints and evidence. You go with Jeff while I call the captain. I'll be right there."

Liz followed Jeff to the manager's office in the back to look at the tapes. She looked at the time, nine o'clock. She wondered how Curtis and Dusty were doing and whether they were still alive. They had been with the traffickers since yesterday afternoon.

Chapter Forty-Seven

"Get up," Jarod shouted, giving Dusty a toe kick in the ribs.

Dusty startled, opening his eyes, looking around, remembering where he was. He jostled Curtis to wake him before Jarod could kick him. Dusty motioned for Curtis to be quiet and pointed.

Pen was sitting with another man in a makeshift office area, murmuring. Still, Dusty caught the words *shipment, Miami, tomorrow* before the other man nodded to Pen that Dusty was watching them.

"Well, well, look, who is awake and ready to work? You boys have some turtles to find today and fast. I won't introduce myself as you don't need to know my name. Pen and Jarod work for me, so you work for me now. Get your asses moving." Latimer whispered something to Pen. Pen tried to argue but dropped it, obviously losing.

Jarod took Curtis by the collar and dragged the boy out of the warehouse. Dusty ran after them shouting, "Hey, where are you taking him? Take me too. I have to go with him."

Curtis swung around and bit Jarod's arm, drawing blood. "You little shit," Jarod swore, letting go of Curtis to wipe the blood off his arm, ready to give Curtis a fist to his face

Dusty came to his rescue, jumping on Jarod and stopping him from slugging Curtis.

"Oh no, you don't hit my cousin, you big bastard." With Dusty holding on, Curtis kicked Jarod in the shin, this time connecting with a resounding thud, and punched the big man in the stomach.

The punch to the stomach had little effect, but the kick hurt like hell, tearing a hole in Jarod's jeans and leaving a four-inch bloody scrape on his leg. Jarod growled and grabbed Dusty off his back, throwing him to the ground. Jarod's face flushed red with rage as he reached for Curtis. He was poised to punch him with a closed fist when Pen shouted. "What the hell is going on out here? Can't you control two young kids?"

Jarod was breathing heavily, trying to control his temper. "They attacked me."

"Looks like they did a good job," Pen said, grinning at the spots of blood on Jarod's arm and the bloody tear in his jeans.

Latimer shuffled out of the warehouse, talking on his phone. "Yes, we'll get the shipment there on time. No, you do not have to come here. Everything's in order. The last of the turtles will be collected today. Yes, I give you my word. The plane will leave here for Miami as planned." Hanging up, Latimer looked at the group standing before him. The last thing he wanted was for Meiling Chang to turn up again. Not much scared him, but she sure as hell did.

"That was Meiling Chang. Her father is expecting a shipment for his auction in Singapore, and I gave him my word that we'll deliver." Latimer looked at the boys and Jarod's injuries, shaking his head. "That means you need to get out there and find me, my damn turtles, now," he shouted. He feared the consequences if he failed to fill the order for this delivery.

Pen jumped into the Jeep, and Jarod forced Dusty and Curtis into the back seat. This time he zip-tied their hands together. He wasn't taking any chances because the boys showed more spirit and desperation.

Dusty shoulder bumped Curtis, "Look at all those airplanes."

"Where the heck are we, Dusty?"

"Darned if I know."

"Shut up and listen," Pen said from his seat in the front, pulling out a map. "We're going to try something different today, boys." We are going to the Little Manatee River State Park. A trail leads to the Little Manatee River. It sounds like a perfect place to hunt for turtles."

Dusty and Curtis looked at each other blankly. "If we've never been there, how do we know where the turtles are?" Curtis asked.

"Because a river is a river, and turtles are turtles. You figure it out." Pen was angry and exhausted. It was much easier when Hap Dunbar organized the kids to find the damn turtles for him. He liked being in charge, not one of the workers.

"We need to eat," Dusty said. He was hungry and knew that Curtis must be as well. They'd had nothing to eat since lunch at school the day before.

"Yeah, no breakfast, no turtles," Curtis echoed, braver than he felt.

Pen was not taking any chances that the boys would refuse to get the turtles he desperately needed. Pen ordered Jarod to drive through a fast-food joint and pick up some breakfast sandwiches for his two captives and coffee for himself and Jarod.

Pen hated wasting time, but the boys shut up while they ate on the way to the park.

Pen paid the fee to enter the park and pulled to the farthest parking spot at the picnic area. The pavilions were deserted so early in the morning. Later it might be a problem.

Jarod motioned for Curtis and Dusty to get out, cutting off the zip ties.

Pen threw them each a large backpack. "We can't have you carrying a bucket of turtles around in a state park, now can we?" he said. "Any turtles you find, you put in the backpack. We'll sort them when we get back."

The boys slipped the packs on, ready to follow the walking trail to the river, when a ranger pulled up.

"Hey, fellas, great time for a hike before it gets too warm. You have enough water with you?"

"Oh sure, my nephews here are old hands and enjoy this out-doors stuff." Pen said.

"Well, enjoy and be safe," the ranger said, but something didn't feel quite right about the group. The boys didn't look happy to be there. One of them was sporting a slight black eye.

He noticed the Asian man, who could be Chinese, wearing

expensive-looking dress shoes and pressed trousers. Not exactly the right outfit for hiking in the woods. But then it took all kinds, didn't it?

It just felt odd. A Chinese uncle with two blond, white kids and a big hulking guy didn't sit right.

"You sure you're OK, boys?"

"Yeah, we're fine. I'll call and tell my mom all about it," Curtis said. He fished Officer Corday's business card out of his pocket and dropped it on the ground, covering it with his shoe. Dusty saw him and tried to distract Pen and Jarod by swatting and yelling about a hornet trying to sting him. Curtis pushed the card to the ranger's boot and prayed. The ranger covered the card with his boot. Curtis nodded, and the ranger nodded back.

"We have to be going," Pen said. "Thank you for checking in with us. We'll be fine."

As the group started down the trail, the ranger thought *Something wasn't right. Not right at all.* Looking at the FWC business card., He'd call the number on the card. As he pulled out his phone, an incoming emergency call sounded and stopped him. The ranger slipped the card into his pocket, jumping in his truck to tackle the emergency at the other end of the park.

Chapter Forty-Eight

Once the ranger was out of sight, Jarod shoved Curtis, sending him tripping to the ground.

"What did you do that for?" Dusty asked.

"Because of this," Jarod answered, holding up his arm with Curtis's teeth marks.

Curtis stood, dusted himself off, and noticed a small side trail leading down to the river. "This way."

Here the tea-colored river moved slowly, barely causing a ripple in the sandy, grassy bottom. The banks were lined with flat woodlands of fetterbush plants and sparkleberry bushes. Tall oaks overhanging the river blocked out the dim early morning sun.

Curtis dropped his pack and walked slowly along the bank, looking for the telltale turtle tracks.

Dusty did the same in the opposite direction, working deeper into the brush. The thought of running from his captors crossed his mind, but he couldn't leave his cousin. They would face whatever was to come together.

Jarod and Pen watched the boys but didn't go with them. They had plans to discuss and didn't want to be overheard.

"This shipment has to be ready to leave first thing tomorrow morning," Pen told Jarod. "Meiling has paid off someone in Miami to load it onto a plane for Singapore, no questions asked."

"What about the kids?" Jarod asked. Even though he bitched

and moaned about them, he had a grudging liking for Curtis and his spirit. Dusty was the thinker and the planner and could be the one to watch. Jarod was of two minds when it came to thoughts of disposing of the boys. He didn't hold with killing children. But what were the consequences for him if he didn't? That Chinese bitch was farther up in the organization than Pen or Latimer. What would he do if she ordered him to kill them?

Dusty returned holding five small box turtles, placing them on the ground at Pen's feet. The turtles began to scurry away. Every turtle was valuable. Latimer would sort them later.

"Put them in the pack. Don't let them get away," Pen shouted. "Get back out there. We need more, much more, and different kinds."

"I can only get what I can find," Dusty growled. He was thinking hard about how to get out of this mess. He could only hope that the ranger would call Officer Corday.

Curtis returned with four cooters in his hands. "I can't do it this way. I saw snappers, but I had no way of catching or holding on to them. This is a silly way of doing things. The bucket was way better."

"Jarod, go with him and get those snapping turtles. They pay big for those. Take the pack and throw any turtles you find in there straight away. Take the other kid with you. I want to be out of here before hikers show up."

An hour later, they were back at the vehicle. A family with three kids was setting up for a picnic at one of the pavilions.

Seeing the family, Jarod shoved Curtis, "Don't get any bright ideas?"

Dusty looked at the family and smiled. Involving them would only bring more trouble. His only hope was in the ranger.

Pen squeezed Dusty by the left arm. The men waved and hustled the boys into the vehicle.

As the Jeep passed the ranger station on the way out, the ranger remembered the strange group and took out the card the young boy had given him.

Punching in the number, he waited for Officer Corday to pick up.

Chapter Forty-Nine

Seth sent a copy of the CCTV footage from the car rental agency to Captain Jacobs, hoping to get a positive ID on who had rented the Jeep. He already suspected that Pham Pen was behind it.

Liz was talking on her phone and excitedly hitting Seth on the leg. Hanging up, she said. "That was a Ranger Garrison at Little Manatee River State Park. He saw the boys."

"What? When?" Seth asked. He looked expectantly at Liz as they drove back from Arcadia.

"This morning, early."

"Why is he only calling you now? How did he get your number?"

"Give me a chance, will you?" Liz said. "Ranger Garrison said he saw the boys with two men, and something felt off. One of the men was Asian, maybe Chinese or Japanese. Anyway, the man said the boys were his nephews. Garrison found that very odd but possible. The smaller kid slipped him my card, which had to be Curtis. Garrison was going to call, but a pygmy rattler bit a hiker, and he had to call for the ambulance and guide the paramedics to the victim. All that made him forget about seeing the boys and the card until he saw their vehicle leaving the park. He dug out my card and called as soon as he could."

"At least we know they're still alive," Seth said. "They must have Dusty and Curtis collecting turtles in that park," Seth said.

"OK, but they still have a problem. The only way to smuggle

the turtles out of the country is by plane. How would you get a load of illegal turtles on a plane and out of the country?"

"You need someone in the cargo terminal to help get past security and onto a plane." Seth was beginning to think this operation was much bigger than they initially thought. The smuggling operation stretched from Arcadia, Florida, to some of the wealthiest buyers in Hong Kong, China, Japan, and beyond.

Every international airport had Customs and Border inspectors. Before loading, they scanned and checked all cargo for drugs and other illegal items, including animals and plants. Someone had to be helping traffic the turtles.

"I'll ask Captain Jacobs to check traffic cameras for that black Jeep. Time is running out. They have to get those turtles out of the country soon."

Liz was punching in Jacob's number when a small passenger jet buzzed overhead. Liz ducked in reflex, "Where the hell did that come from?"

"It's still pretty rural around out here. Some of the cattle ranches and citrus growers have their own turf airstrips. I didn't think any of them could handle a jet?" Seth said. But something was trying to surface from the depths of his memory.

Liz finished her call with the captain, and he agreed to check the traffic cameras. "There are a couple main roads they could use to get back to the Arcadia area. If that's where they are heading."

"I've been thinking about that," Seth said, pulling onto SR 17. "They rented their vehicle in Arcadia. How did they get to Arcadia?"

"You're right," Liz answered. "Where are we headed, by the way?"

"I thought we would let Mrs. Dunbar and the Stirlings know the boys have been seen alive."

Chapter Fifty

Holler was lying on the porch when Liz and Seth pulled up in front of Mrs. Dunbar's house in Nocatee. The old dog stood up, wagging his tail, his deep hound bark announcing their arrival. He had a bandage wrapped around his middle to protect his cracked and bruised ribs. Walking stiffly down the steps, he sniffed Seth and Liz, licking their hands in turn. A sad look in his eyes asked where Curtis was.

"Sorry, pal. We're trying to bring him home." Seth said to the dog.

Mrs. Dunbar looked out the window before opening the door. "Come in. Have you heard anything? Please don't tell me it's bad news." Lorraine Dunbar was on the verge of tears.

"It's not bad news. Let's have a seat." Liz guided the woman to the shabby living room. "Has your husband come home yet? I was hoping to meet with him."

"He called to say he was on his way. He said he had to wait to borrow some money from his boss for gas. I don't know if I can believe him or not. He hardly sends anything home for the kids and me. He didn't have the money to bury his own father." Lorraine was raging at her husband. "I could strangle him with my bare hands. I'm so mad at him right now." Her hands clenched tight.

The back door opened, and Mrs. Chavez came hustling in. "Have you found them? Are they safe?"

"Hello again, Mrs. Chavez," Seth said, eliciting a smile from the older Hispanic woman. "We were about to tell Mrs. Dunbar that a ranger at Little Manatee River Park saw the boys in the company of two men this morning. We are trying to find where they might have headed from there. The FWC and the Sheriff's Departments are using traffic cameras to spot their vehicle. The men who took the boys are crossing county lines and making it difficult to coordinate these efforts."

"I understand," Mrs. Chavez said, reaching out to take Lorraine's hand. "Have you told the Stirlings yet?"

"No, we came here first," Liz said. "We'll call them, but we wanted to tell you in person."

"Thank you. I appreciate that more than you know."

The roar of a loud truck passing on the road halted their conversation.

"Damn, that sounded like a plane landing on top of us," Liz said.

"That's Henry Ruiz. He has a haulage company and brings his truck home sometimes," Mrs. Chavez laughed, "I've lived here so long it doesn't bother me anymore."

Seth was trying to dig up that memory. It was bubbling to the surface. "Do you know if any ranchers or grove owners have a small jet plane? One flew pretty low when we were coming here this morning."

"Oh, my dear, there is a municipal airport in Arcadia. It can handle smaller jets. It used to be a WWII training base in the old days. They used to call it Aviation city back then. There are still some hangers and a small passenger terminal out there. It's only bad when there are storms in the area, and the planes have to fly in low."

Seth jumped up and took the woman by the shoulders, "Mrs. Chavez, I could kiss you." He planted a kiss on her wrinkled cheek. The woman had just given them the key they needed to save the boys.

"Ladies, we have to be going. Mrs. Dunbar. We're closer to bringing the boys home. Mrs. Chavez, save me some empanadas. We will be back soon, I hope." Seth said, tipping his cap.

Chapter Fifty-One

"We have to call Captain Jacobs and fill him in on all we have learned," Liz said.

"I don't know why I didn't think of that airport before. Our history teacher told us about it. Most of these small training bases were decommissioned after the war, and the developers moved in over time. Arcadia manages to hold out and has some private air traffic to stay in business."

"I'm guessing that is how our traffickers landed in the area and smuggled the turtles out."

"Let's do a run out to the airport and have a look around. You call Captain Jacobs. Maybe we can see the boys."

"What are we going to do if we do see them?" Liz asked.

"I think I will have to ask the great Breathmaker of the Seminoles to guide us."

Seth punched in the GPS and asked for the Arcadia Municipal Airport. He was thrilled when the map showed up on his screen.

Liz called Jacobs, telling him what they had found out. He cautioned them about going but understood the need to see if the boys were there.

Hanging up, Liz reached across and took Seth's hand in hers. This was not the first time they had run into danger together. Last time she was almost eaten by an alligator when she was knocked into an alligator holding pen before Seth managed to drag her out in time.

Being an FWC officer was not for the faint-hearted. It took guts and determination. It also helped if you didn't mind getting covered in all kinds of horrible smelly crap.

Seth noticed the smile on Liz's face.

"What has you so happy this morning?"

"I was thinking about the time that gator almost got me at the alligator farm."

"Almost being some alligator's lunch makes you happy?"

"No, but you saving me does. I love my work, even though it is sometimes dangerous, and I love being with you. It's the best life ever." Liz continued to smile when Seth brought her hand up and kissed it.

"Best life ever," Seth echoed.

SR 17 took them directly back to Arcadia. Staying on SR 70, they looked for Airport Rd. Working slowly down the rutted road, they noticed a road to their left leading past an aviation school to the terminal and warehouse buildings.

They parked their truck in the trees behind the flight school and walked the rest of the way. "No point announcing ourselves before we have to," Seth said, quietly closing the door.

Liz nudged Seth and nodded to the Jeep beside the nearest warehouse. Behind it was a flatbed truck.

Pointing to a window, Seth put his hands together for Liz to use to step up and look inside. Liz put her boot in Seth's hand so he could lift her. Holding on to the window edge, she was able to peer inside.

After a few seconds, Liz came down. "The boys are there with three men, Pham Pen, that big guy with the tattoos we saw before, and another man. There are four wading pools with different species of turtles in them. I saw a soft shell, box turtles, a few cooters, and common snappers. Some are too small to be sure what they are. They have plastic boxes lined up on folding tables."

"They must be getting ready to move. We have to call Captain Jacobs and alert the DeSoto Sheriff's Office now."

Seth put his head around the building in time to see a flashy Maserati sports car drive up and a striking Chinese woman emerge and enter the warehouse.

Pulling back to Liz, Seth said, "See if you can open that window a crack to hear what they're saying."

He boosted Liz up to the window again. Liz used a pocket knife to pry the window loose and push it open slightly. Ducking down, she heard the group speaking quickly. The woman was speaking English with heavy Chinese accents.

"The shipment goes out tomorrow morning at eight o'clock to Miami." Liz heard the woman saying. "I already have it on the runway schedule, so don't mess it up."

"What about the boys?" Jarod asked.

"That is not my problem. Getting the turtles to my father is my problem. Making it happen is your problem. We all have problems that must be dealt with, so deal with them."

"You can't expect me to kill a couple kids," Jarod said, raising his voice. Pen gripped his arm and stopped him from advancing on Meiling.

Meiling dropped her hand, revealing the five-inch-long slender rapier thin knife she had taken from the coils of her hair.

Latimer stood beside Meiling, "I can take care of the problem.

The boys can help sort and get the shipment ready. Then we can decide how to silence them permanently."

"We do not give second chances, Latimer. Get the job done." The unsaid *or else* hung in the air. Meiling walked by the wading pools on her way out the door assaying the turtles there.

After Meiling left, Jarod turned on Latimer. "You must feed those kids if you want them to help sort the turtles. You can't let them go hungry."

"Personally, I don't give a shit about those kids. After the shipment is sent out, they are expendable. Order them a pizza and get it delivered. Get some water and some soft drinks too. Get enough for all of us. It's going to be a long night."

Dusty and Curtis huddled in a corner, hot, exhausted, and hungry. They were out of earshot of their captor and could not hear their conversation, but Curtis bumped Dusty and lifted his chin slightly to the window. Dusty saw Liz at the window and nodded.

Liz nodded back before slipping down and motioning Seth to follow her away.

Once clear of the building, Liz said. "They're shipping the turtles out early tomorrow morning."

"What about the boys?"

"That's the bad part. That Chinese woman told the men to deal with them. They are planning on killing them. The boys saw me and know we are trying to get to them."

"Let's make those calls now. We have to get things moving and fast."

Sitting in their vehicle, hidden by trees and brush, Seth and Liz informed the appropriate authorities. The FWC and the DeSoto sheriffs would be standing ready to rescue Curtis and Dusty and arrest the traffickers.

"We can't take the time to go home and back again. How do you feel about staying here tonight?" Seth asked.

"I was hoping you would say that. I want to stay close to the boys just in case."

"You think that pizza guy could find us back here in the trees and deliver to us as well?"

"Very funny. Lucky for you, I have some energy bars and a couple bottles of water," Liz said, reaching into the back seat and pulling out an emergency backpack she kept stowed back there.

Seth called his ranger friend Darrell at Manasota State Park to take care of Nokosi until they returned. Darrell served at the park when Seth was the head ranger. Darrell called him Chief then, and the nickname had stuck. They had remained friends after Seth left to become a Florida Fish and Wildlife Officer. Darrell was married to his then-girlfriend Marcia now and expecting their first child.

Every time Seth called on Darrell to help with Nokosi, he wondered if Liz would ever give in and marry him and give him a family. He hated to admit it, but he was jealous of Darrell.

He was hanging up when the Maserati flew past them again, heading away from the airport.

"I wonder where she's going in such a hurry?" Seth asked.

"We need to find out who the hell she is and what she has to do with all this. Pham Pen seemed to be afraid of her," Liz said.

"We'll find out, and we will bring those kids home safe."

Chapter Fifty-Two

A half-hour later, a car with a pizza delivery sign on the top pulled up to the warehouse door.

Jarod answered the knock and paid the driver cash. Pen helped carry in three large pizzas, two six-packs of soft drinks, and a 24-pack of water.

"Hell, you think this is enough?" Jarod asked.

"Just shut up and put it over there," Latimer said, indicating a table.

Pen had been quiet since Meiling had appeared on the scene with deadly orders. He knew that he was as expendable as the two young kids were. Jarod would be too. There would be no loose ends for the Chinese masters.

"Kids," Latimer called. "Get your asses over here and get something to eat. We have work to do."

Dusty poked Curtis to wake him up, "Come on and get some pizza."

"I don't want pizza. I wanna go home," Curtis moaned. White streaks ran down his face from where his tears had washed away the dust and grime.

"You saw Officer Corday," Dusty whispered. "She's out there trying to figure a way to get us out of here. We have to play along until she can come an' get us."

That seemed to satisfy Curtis, and the boys made their way past the pool containing the turtles to the table. Dusty grabbed two slices and a drink and made Curtis take a slice and something to drink. "You have got to eat."

Latimer noticed Curtis not wanting to eat., "What's the matter with him?"

"He's afraid and wants to go home. What are you going to do with us?" Dusty dared to ask. A vision of the dead man they found in the woods with a bullet hole in his head flashed through his brain. Was that going to be their fate?

"That kinda depends. You sort the turtles and get them packaged for me, and we'll see. I might give you a job in my organization." Latimer laughed as he took his plate and walked back to his desk. He didn't give a damn what happened to the kids so long as he didn't get killed.

"What is going on?" Jarod asked Pen. "I thought you were the big man in charge, and I haven't heard a word from you since that Chinese bitch showed up."

"You don't understand. Don't underestimate Meiling. She is very dangerous. Cross her, and you die."

"What the hell did you get me into?"

"Her father is the one calling the shots and is head of one of the biggest criminal syndicates in China. The Mafia and the Russian mob look like Boy Scouts compared to them."

"You said we were trafficking a few turtles to Asia for the pet trade. Not hundreds for an illegal auction in Singapore." Jarod was pacing, looking at the boys every few seconds. "I killed an old man, their grandfather, for a few fucking turtles. This is so messed up." Jarod threw his paper plate with a half-eaten slice across the table.

"Shut up before Latimer hears you. We get the job done and hope we get out of this alive." Pen muttered, even though he had his doubts.

Jarod looked across the room at Latimer sitting smugly with his feet propped up on his desk, stuffing pizza in his face.

Jarod watched Curtis and Dusty crouched by the wall. All his life Jarod had considered himself the tough guy, the rogue, the gun for hire. He had done some terrible things, but enough was enough. There was a line he wouldn't cross, and killing kids was it.

That was one rule he never broke. He wasn't about to break it now. Curtis and Dusty were in over their heads; that was their grandfather's fault, but they didn't deserve to die.

Latimer wiped off his hands and started over. "OK, let's get this show on the road. You boys, get over here while I tell you what to do."

Added to the boxes were piles of socks of different sizes and rolls of cotton fiber. On the floor, bags of Styrofoam peanuts were stacked under the tables. "Listen to me. You go to the pools. Take only one kind of turtle out and put it in one of the boxes. In the next box, you put a layer of peanuts. Put a turtle from the first box in a sock and wrap it in a damp piece of the cotton roll. Make sure the turtles can't move around. We don't want them damaged. Then put more peanuts on top and close the box. Write how many turtles are in the box and what kind with a marker, then move to the next box."

The boys spent the next couple of hours packing the turtles, with Dusty marking the containers. Dusty counted two hundred and five turtles of different kinds.

They wrapped each one carefully and packed them like sandwiches, one after the other. They had to ensure the turtles were in their shells, and some didn't want to go. It was frustrating work, and the turtles would bite and snap. Curtis received a couple good bites, and his fingers were bleeding.

"Now for the prize." Latimer shoved Curtis towards the large pool in the corner of the warehouse. "See what you can do with this guy here. He needs special care."

Curtis looked down into the jaws of a juvenile alligator-snapping turtle. The turtle hissed and tried to claw his way out of the pool but kept slipping back down.

Eyes wide, Curtis turned, staring up at Latimer. "What am I supposed to do with him?"

Curtis weighed in at eighty pounds. Ten pounds more than the monster he was supposed to move.

"You are out of your mind," Jarod yelled, coming to Curtis's rescue. "You can't expect him to move that thing."

"OK, you do it. There is a dog cage over there to put him in."

Latimer stopped and thought a moment. "No. Wait, do it in the morning. I don't want him stressed out," Latimer said.

"You don't want him stressed? What about the rest of us and what you're doing to these kids?"

"What the hell do these kids mean to you anyway? You going soft?"

"No, I just don't hold with hurting kids." Jarod strode off, mumbling. He was growing upset with Pen for withholding information about the operation, and he would not kill these two kids.

Jarod noticed Pen sitting at a table, staring into space.

"Again, what's up with you? You haven't said a word in hours. You are beginning to piss me off."

"Working for Meiling's father was supposed to be easy money. Catch a few turtles and put them on a plane. I didn't expect her to show up."

"So, my badass boss is not such a badass after all. Is that it? I beat up an old man, killed him for you. I terrified two young boys for you. I hope that crazy bitch does kill you."

Chapter Fifty-Three

The cloud-streaked sky towards the East Coast of Florida was exploding with magenta and gold when Liz shook Seth. The sports car was back.

Liz's phone vibrated. The captain's ID showed on the screen.

"Yes, Captain, we're here. The Maserati is back. I think they're getting ready to move." Liz listened for a few minutes before hanging up.

"Captain said the sheriff's deputies are surrounding the airport. The FWC will take the lead in securing the warehouse because of the threat to wildlife. Officers Jessup and Garcia are here to help as well. The captain wants you and I to get the boys out. I have no idea how we're going to do that."

Liz looked over at Seth. He was sitting there with his eyes closed, fingers drumming on the steering wheel.

"What the hell are you doing?"

"Thinking. We have civilian clothes in the back, right?"

"Yeah? They were going to Goodwill, but I haven't had time to drop them off." Liz was wondering where this was going.

"I'll tell you as we change out of these uniforms."

Digging in the back, Seth found the clothes and threw the bag on the ground. They quickly changed and tucked their guns into the back waistband of their pants. Praying they would not need them.

Approaching the warehouse, Seth and Liz could make out the other FWC officers converging. The sky was lightening, and birds were flying overhead. Egrets called as they left their roosts.

Seth lifted Liz to the window, held her there for a few seconds, and let her down.

"Curtis and Dusty are asleep by the far wall," Liz told him. "Pen and his man, I heard him called Jarod, are loading the boxes with the turtles in heavy cardboard containers with airholes labeled *live animals*. They are loading boxes onto the truck outside by a side door in the corner I didn't see before. The other man and the Chinese woman are arguing over something."

"OK, just play along, and we just might make it out alive and with the boys."

"Oh, I love role play."

Chapter Fifty-Four

Talking loudly, Seth barged into the warehouse. "I tell you, Tracy, this place will be perfect. We can put the plane in here and still have room for a little rec area for the gang to hang out."

A shocked Latimer braced himself in front of Seth and Liz. "Who the hell are you? What are you doing in my warehouse?"

Looking just as shocked, Seth answered, "The woman at the terminal said this place would be vacant today. We're just coming to check it out. You know, see if our stuff will fit."

"Yeah, Lou and I have this neat little Piper Cub that needs a new home, and this will work fine. We moved here from New York and want to be able to vacay in the islands if you know what I mean?" Liz wished she had some chewing gum to snap for effect. She hoped she was getting the New York accent right.

"You know. Fly over to Jamaica, man. Pick up a little rum. Fly back under the radar." Liz put her arms out and pretended to fly like a plane.

Latimer looked at her like she had a few screws loose. Which was the effect she was hoping for.

Seth was looking around. Latimer and Meiling were not happy with the new visitors. Pen and Jarod had stopped packing up the turtles to watch.

The boys were awake now. Curtis recognized Liz and was going to call out, but Dusty stopped him. "Shush, don't give them away.

They're here for us. Come on, but don't say a word."

Dusty guided Curtis close to where Liz and Seth were standing, talking to Latimer.

"Hi boys, you enjoy flying?" Liz asked. "We've got a plane outside. You want to see it? I could give you a ride."

"That would be neat. What do you think, Curtis?" Dusty said.

"Yeah, I'd like that," Curtis said, unsure of what was happening.

Latimer went to grab Dusty, but he danced out of the way, "The boys don't have time and are not flying anywhere. They have some work to do."

"Sure, I understand." Seth took over. "How about the boys take a little peek at the plane and come right back? We can take them up another day. I'm sure the woman at the terminal will be around shortly, so we can sign the lease agreement anyway. She was going to meet us here. I can see how busy you are packing to leave and all."

Latimer shrugged, shaking his head. He hated complications, and having the woman who ran the airport come by and see what they were doing was a big complication. Meiling was sitting by his desk, playing with one of her slender knives.

"Five minutes," Latimer agreed. "Jarod, go with them and make sure they come right back. You hear me? Right back."

He was taking a huge risk letting Dusty and Curtis leave the building, but he had no choice if the airport manager was coming. Latimer had to make it look like everything was on the up and up.

Liz bent over between Dusty and Curtis. "You are not coming back. Do as I say, and everything will be fine." She walked the boys slowly out of the warehouse, followed by Seth.

"You're going to love this plane. It's called *Homeward Bound,*" Seth said for the boys to hear. Dusty bumped Curtis and smiled.

Latimer stopped Jarod, "You make sure those boys come back. Do whatever you have to do to Tracy and Lou if they make a fuss."

Scowling, Latimer walked back to Meiling. Watching her play with her knife gave him the creeps. "Can you please put that thing away and help get this shipment packed up and on the truck? The plane will be on the runway any minute."

"Why did you let those kids go? They were insurance. They also know too much."

"Don't worry. I told Jarod to bring them back. We can't afford to raise any red flags when we are so close."

Chapter Fifty-Five

Seth led the boys out of the warehouse, with Liz and Jarod following. Seth wanted to get clear of the building before the deputies and his colleagues moved in.

Seth was hustling Dusty and Curtis away when Jarod took hold of Curtis's arm and pulled him back.

"Hey, where's this plane of yours?" Jarod shouted, holding on to Curtis and dragging him back towards the warehouse.

"It's parked nearby on the taxiway," Liz said, pushing Dusty behind her back. "You can't see it from here."

"Lying bastards." Jarod picked up Curtis. "You're coming with me," he said, rushing back to the warehouse. Curtis bawled, kicking and screaming, "Let me go, let me go."

Bursting in the door, he yelled, "It's a setup. They were taking the kids."

"What the hell," Latimer shouted back. "Check outside. There could be more of them. How did they find the boys? The FWC or the sheriff could be on the way."

Pen began walking slowly to the door while they were distracted, hoping no one would notice. He was ready to run. Unfortunately, Meiling was watching and caught him sneaking off.

"Mr. Pen, leaving us so soon?" Meiling stood and juggled her knife in her hands. A cruel smile danced on her lips.

Pen stopped, "I was just checking outside to see if I could spot anyone." His heart was ready to explode, feeling her eyes on him and seeing the lie on his face. Twenty steps to the door, he could escape all this. It wasn't his plan to work for a Chinese mobster. When Meiling didn't say anything, he took another step, took another breath, and… bolted for the door.

Pen dropped to the concrete floor. A slender five-inch knife embedded in his back had severed his spinal cord. Bright red spread out to stain Pen's shirt, running across the concrete floor. Meiling leaned over the body and tugged her weapon out, cleaning the blood off on Pen's shirt, laughing to herself, a maniacal grin on her face. She had enjoyed the kill.

Curtis was stunned. His mouth hung open in a silent scream.

"You are beyond crazy," Jarod mumbled. At that point, he realized that Meiling was a deranged psycho.

He pushed Curtis back., "Stay here, and don't say a word."

"You got any bright ideas on how we are going to get out of this?" Latimer said to Meiling.

"We are going to finish loading the shipment. My father demands it."

"Are you nuts? FWC probably surrounds the building, and the police are shutting down the airport. There is no place to go."

Meiling rose from her seat and strolled slowly to Latimer. She ran one of her metal-tipped red lacquered nails down the side of his neck along his jugular vein and laughed. "I never disappoint my father."

Chapter Fifty-Six

Liz crept back to the building and opened the side door a crack to see Latimer arguing with Meiling. Jarod was standing there watching, his back to Curtis. Silently threading her way through the cardboard boxes, she got close enough to throw a small stone she found on the floor at Curtis.

Curtis was startled and almost cried out when he saw her. Liz put her finger to her lips and motioned him to come to her and stay low. Curtis, at first, shook his head no. He was afraid to move.

Liz beckoned him to her again, watching for Latimer and the others. Finally, Curtis moved, scurrying across to Liz.

"Be very quiet. Dusty is outside waiting for you."

Liz pushed Curtis through the door and was about to follow him when Latimer shouted, "Hey, what the hell? Go after them."

Jarod fell through the door in pursuit and took hold of Liz, throwing her to the ground. In that instant, he heard the click of a gun pointed at his head. Jarod closed his eyes, clenched his fists, and muttered, "Shit."

"Hands on your head, big boy," Officer Garcia said. "Officer Jessup, would you please do the honors."

"Be happy too, boss," Jessup said, grinning.

Liz was on her feet, Glock in hand, as Officer Jessup made his first arrest, putting cuffs on Jerod and walking him to a waiting vehicle.

"Where's Seth?" Liz asked.

"Oh, he's around here somewhere," Officer Garcia said with a knowing look.

"Oh shit, not again," Liz groaned

Liz stepped back to the side door and saw Latimer and Meiling. Latimer was yelling, "What the hell is taking him so long? One skinny kid and woman can't be that much trouble."

Liz grinned as she saw Seth walking in the front door of the warehouse, followed by several FWC officers in Kevlar vests and helmets carrying assault weapons.

Latimer pushed Meiling out of the way to run for the side door, but Liz stood in his way.

He turned and ran in a circle looking for a way out. Meiling advanced on him. "Get away from me, you psycho. It's over." Latimer said, backing away from Meiling. His eyes darted from her to the officers fanning out over the room. He was trying to decide which was the worse fate.

Seth called out, "You can't go anywhere. Give it up. Latimer, you and your friend here are under arrest for wildlife trafficking."

Meiling stood her ground, hands on hips, chin in the air, planting her feet for a fight.

"My name is Meiling Yang. My father is a powerful man in Singapore. He has many important connections. You will see. I will do no time in your American jail."

Latimer hung his head, "No time in jail, huh? I'm tired of your shit." Latimer took Meiling by surprise, half dragging, half carrying, and tossed her into the pool with the alligator snapping turtle.

His eyes glared down at her as she struggled to regain footing on the slippery surface.

The massive turtle, hungry and angry, took its revenge. Opening its powerful jaws and with one thousand pounds of pressure, it clamped down on Meiling's shoulder, cracking through bone and sinew. Her subclavian artery ruptured, spraying drops of red like rain. Her screams echoed through the warehouse.

Liz closed her eyes, blocking out the horror, and held her breath for a split second before standing beside Seth. Her gun pointed at

Latimer. "You heard the officer. You are under arrest for trafficking wildlife. I think we can add murder to that charge and maybe kidnapping."

"I didn't kidnap those kids. That was Pen's idea. It was the only way to collect enough turtles for the shipment and get that bitch off our backs."

Latimer gave up without a struggle as Seth cuffed him. Liz took one arm and Seth the other, walking Latimer out of the warehouse past the waiting FWC vehicles.

Jarod sat in one and turned his head away when Latimer passed.

After locking Latimer in one of the sheriff's vehicles, Seth took Liz in his arms, "You think we can go home now? I need something besides granola bars."

"I think I can manage that and maybe a bit more," Liz said, taking his lips with hers and not caring who was watching.

"OK, break it up, you two," Captain Jacobs said. "I have someone here who wants to see you both."

Dusty and Curtis came over, tears glistening in the boys' eyes.

"We can't thank you enough for coming to help us. I thought for sure they were going to kill us." Dusty said.

Curtis stood there looking at Liz for a moment and then flung himself at her, wrapping his arms around her. He looked up into her face, whispering, "Thank you."

"How would you boys like to go home now?" Seth asked.

"Yes, please," Dusty said as Curtis nodded.

Liz and Seth received permission from Jacobs to take the boys home. Questions and statements would wait until tomorrow.

On the way to their vehicle, Seth let the boys walk a bit ahead.

"We'll call their parents on the way to let them know we're coming," Seth said. "It's going to be a busy few days relocating all those turtles. I'll ask Officer Garcia to have Jessup help him with some of that."

Captain Jacobs came over, "I will be looking to track down whoever was assisting the traffickers in Miami. I can get Customs and Border Patrol to help with that."

Seth and Liz walked silently side-by-side for a few steps before Liz spoke again, giggling, "I think you might be right about Curtis having a little crush on me."

"Well, I know someone who has a massive crush on you."

Playing innocent, Liz acted surprised, "Really, who?"

"Me. and I'm going to prove it to you when we get home."

Chapter Fifty-Seven

Lorraine Dunbar hugged Curtis so hard he thought his bones would break. He had never seen his mother cry so much or been so happy to see him all at the same time. Even his little sisters ran to hug him when Seth and Liz dropped him off.

Mrs. Chavez waved and watched from her house. Even a close neighbor knew when not to intrude. She would go over later with some baked goods.

Even his dad was home, standing on the porch, not moving or saying anything. Curtis felt something was wrong but put it out of his mind when Holler bowled him over, covering him with sloppy kisses, and attaching himself to Curtis.

Dusty's parents were more reserved. His mother cried, dabbing her eyes with a handkerchief and hugging him. His father patted him on the shoulder and welcomed him back.

Seth watched the two family groups. One was struggling to survive but full of love and caring. The other was financially stable but lacked the unconditional love of the first family. He finally had a glimpse of what Liz had been through in her life. Liz was torn between the love and care her father gave her and her social-climbing mother, where outward appearance meant everything.

The sheriff's vehicles left Curtis and Dusty waving them off.

Next to leave were the Stirlings. Mike Stirling came over to Seth and Liz, "I'm making some changes and going to try and do more with Dusty and Curtis. Maybe they can teach me some outdoor stuff they like so much." Mike extended his hand to Seth.

"I had a talk with Lorraine about working at the bank. I should have done it before now. Mary has been after me about it for ages. It's about time I stepped up."

Seth took Mike's hand, "I'm sure she'll do a great job."

The Stirlings drove off with Dusty yelling out the window, "See ya later, Curtis."

Seth and Liz were climbing into their vehicle when Curtis ran up and threw his arms around Liz again. He looked up at Seth, saying, "She's special, you know."

"Yeah, I know."

Seth bent down and asked the boy, "I almost forgot. Do you still think you want to be an FWC officer?"

"More than ever. You guys are the best."

"How would you like to come with Liz and me to see a bear released in the Three Lakes wilderness Area tomorrow? That is if your mom and dad say it's OK."

Curtis's mouth dropped open. Turning to his mom, "Mom, can I, can I? Please, I've never seen a bear."

He looked up at his dad, standing silent on the porch, and then back to his mom. Curtis was confused about who was making the decisions now that his dad was home.

"We have to do it anyway," Liz said. "Curtis would be along for the ride. It will be a fantastic experience for him if he is considering joining the FWC, Mrs. Dunbar."

"Please, Please, Mom," Curtis pleaded.

"We have another special treat for him," Liz said. "We are stopping at Seth's parents on the way back. Curtis was asking about Seth being a Seminole. Seth's parents live on the Seminole Reservation in Hillsborough and are having a dance. Curtis could meet members of the tribe and maybe even learn some of the dances like I did."

Curtis suddenly looked sad and unexcited.

"Curtis, what's the matter?" Liz asked, noticing the sudden change in the boy's mood.

Mrs. Dunbar noticed, too, "Honey, what's wrong?"

"Well, I just got home. Holler won't understand if I up and take off again so soon. I really want to go, but I don't want to leave Holler."

"Then, we'll just have to take Holler with us," Seth said, looking at Mr. and Mrs. Dunbar for permission.

Mrs. Dunbar asked, "When are you planning this trip?"

"We will leave tomorrow morning. It might be midnight by the time we brought Curtis back. I know you just got him back, but an opportunity like this might not happen again for a long time."

"Please, Mom," Curtis said.

Mrs. Dunbar looked back over her shoulder at her husband. He nodded, OK.

"I know you will take care of him. His dad and I have some talking to do. Better Curtis doesn't hear it anyway."

Seth knew that a talk like that could go either way. He hoped his dad would be around more after all Curtis had experienced. Curtis was a sensitive kid with potential and needed the help and support of his family.

"Liz and I will pick Curtis and Holler up about eight o'clock. Be sure to pack some food for Holler. It will be a long day."

Liz took Seth's hand as they drove back to their home in Sarasota. "I'm so glad that is over. They'll release the turtles back into the reserves and parks where they belong. Curtis will get the help he needs with his reading. Mrs. Dunbar will get a position at the bank where she can make a decent wage to help her family."

"I'm wondering what will happen between Mr. and Mrs. Dunbar," Seth said.

"That's why they agreed to let Curtis come with us for the day. That conversation might get a bit heated."

"You could be right."

Liz's phone rang. She reluctantly dropped Seth's hand to answer the call from Captain Jacobs.

Hanging up, she turned to Seth. "You are not going to believe this. Latimer has bailed out already."

"How the hell did that happen?" Seth asked

"Some swanky high-priced defense lawyer came in, argued down the bail, and paid to have him let out with a promise to appear."

"Well, we know that is not going to happen. Latimer knows too much about the operation. He's going to disappear one way or another."

"The captain also said they are watching the Miami airport cargo area," Liz said. "Someone there was helping to smuggle the turtles out of the country. He's sending some of our officers to help the Border Patrol agriculture specialist that works there. It's a coordinated effort to prevent another shipment they may try to ship out.

"Do you think Latimer is heading for Miami?"

"It could be he's hoping that whoever he was working for will get him out of the country. That Chinese woman was over Latimer. Someone sent her here. The head of the organization in Singapore. We can't do anything about that."

Nokosi chose that moment to let them know he needed his supper.

"I'll fix his supper. Liz offered. "You call Darrell and see if he can check on Nokosi tomorrow. I'd take him with us, but the truck is not big enough for two big dogs."

"You've got that right. Might be fun to see those two dogs together sometime, though." Seth chuckled, reaching for his phone.

Chapter Fifty-Eight

Bright and early at 8 am the following day, Seth and Liz pulled up in front of the Dunbar house to find Curtis and Holler waiting on the porch.

Hearing the truck, Lorraine Dunbar came out to greet them and see her son off. Her eyes were red-rimmed from crying.

Liz approached the young mother, "Are you alright?"

"Yeah, my husband and I got into it a bit last night." Lorraine walked to the other end of the yard, signaling Liz to follow. Seth was helping Curtis to load his things into the truck.

"My husband has confessed that he has a gambling problem." Lorraine started talking. "That's why he's not been sending much money home. It was tough for him to admit he had a problem but losing his father and almost losing Curtis was the wake-up call he needed. We talked and cried all night. He'll go to a program at our local church. The feed store in Arcadia has a full-time job opening, and he's going to apply. He has a good chance of getting it. Officer Corday, things are finally turning around for us. I can't believe it," Lorraine said, catching a tear running down her cheek.

"I'm so happy for all of you."

"Liz, we have to go," Seth called.

"Yes, I'm afraid it's a long drive. We will bring Curtis home later this evening. If you need anything at all, give me a call."

"Thank you, Officer Corday. Curtis admires you and Officer Grayson very much." Lorraine glanced back at the house. "This will give my husband and me some time to discuss things. He's too young to understand much of what has happened between his father and me."

"We're happy to have him and Holler. We do need to get moving." Liz couldn't resist hugging Mrs. Dunbar.

Liz looked over at Seth with Curtis and Holler already in the back seat, ready to go.

She briefly considered whether she would ever have a family in the back seat waiting for her one day. Deciding to sell her condo was a big step in that direction. Could she make the biggest decision and say yes to the man she loved?

Chapter Fifty-Nine

Mr. Garrett was waiting for them when they pulled into the gravel yard of the honey farm. "Hi, there, officers."

"Mr. Garrett, I'd like you to meet a future FWC officer, Curtis Dunbar. He's doing a ride along with us today to see this bear of yours get relocated," Seth said.

"Pleased to meet you, young man. These officers do a fine job. I hope you do become one of them someday."

"Thank you, sir. I hope so, too," Curtis replied. Curtis was overjoyed that Seth had introduced him as a future FWC officer. He could already see himself in uniform doing the exciting things they did.

"Who have you got with you?" Mr. Garrett said, patting Holler.

"This is my dog, Holler. He's my best friend."

"Well, I'm sure he is. Let's just keep him away from the beehives, and he'll be fine. Dogs and bees don't always get along."

"Let's take that bear off your hands," Liz said. "He's back here," Garrett said, walking to the back of his

house, where he kept his hives.

Behind his home, the beekeeper had forty hives lined up in wooden boxes. The boxes were piled three or four high and buzzing with activity. Some others were smashed and scattered in pieces on the ground.

"I heard the trap door bang about midnight and couldn't sleep a wink with all the commotion that bear was making. He sure didn't like the idea of being in that trap. He's quieted down some now."

A few yards ahead sat a large green cylindrical steel trap on wheels with a very angry bear inside.

Holler sniffed the air and edged closer to Curtis, whining at the smell.

"You can take a look but don't touch the trap, and don't put your fingers in any of the holes," Seth cautioned Curtis.

Curtis took small slow steps, peeking through one of the side holes. The young bear must have sensed his presence and lunged and roared, lunging toward Curtis. Frightened, the boy stumbled back and fell to the ground, "Jeez, he's huge. I'm glad he's in there, and I'm out here. He sure does smell bad."

Seth laughed and helped the boy up. "He sure does. I'll get the truck hooked up. Liz, maybe you and Mr. Garrett can show Curtis the hives," Seth said, knowing it would take several minutes to accomplish, and Curtis might as well learn something in the meantime.

"How about I take Holler with me so he doesn't disturb the bees and get stung?"

"That might be a good idea, Curtis," Liz agreed, taking Holler's leash from Curtis and handing it to Seth.

Both Curtis and Holler looked unsure, but in the end, Curtis said., "It's OK, Holler. I'll be right there."

Holler walked away with Seth but kept looking back at Curtis. Seth put Holler in the truck and hooked the trap to the trailer hitch on the back of his truck.

Mr. Garrett showed Liz and Curtis the bear damage.

"Wow, that bear did all this?" Curtis said, seeing twenty or more wooden hives in pieces on the ground. "Did the bear eat the bees too?"

"Some, yes. If the queen survived, they would start a new colony. You can see I've built a couple new hives for them. I'll look for a queen in one of the old hives, and the bees will follow her."

"Before you go, I'll give you a book on bees and a jar of honey. Would you like that?"

"Yes, please," Curtis said. He would ask his new teacher, Nancy

Taylor, to help him with it. It was the first book he really wanted to read.

Seth was ready to leave, and the bear was not happy about being jostled. "Liz, Curtis, it's time we were going," Seth called.

As soon as Curtis got back in the truck, Holler gave him a big sloppy kiss. Mr. Garret handed him the book and a jar of honey.

"It's orange blossom honey. I know you'll like it."

"Thanks, Mr. Garrett," Curtis said, already flipping pages in the book.

Seth shook hands with Mr. Garrett as Liz climbed in, buckling her seat belt and ensuring that Curtis did the same.

Pulling out onto SR 17, Curtis looked back at the trap with the bear inside. He smiled and waved at the people in the cars they passed as they pointed at the bear. It was one of his best days ever. It helped to cancel out all the bad stuff of the last few days.

Chapter Sixty

It was a long drive to the Three Lakes Wilderness Area seventy miles south of Kissimmee in Central Florida, which would be followed by another long drive back to Tampa and his parent's house.

They checked in at the gate and drove back to the limited access area where few people were allowed to go. Seth's truck and the trap bounced down the rutted track to a deeply forested area on the edge of a flat prairie. On the way, Liz pointed out Florida scrub jays and red-cockaded woodpeckers making pine trees their homes. A couple sandhill cranes wandered across and slowed their progress. Curtis was fascinated. His head swiveled and took it all in. As much as he wandered in the woods at home, he saw things he had never noticed before.

Seth backed his truck with the trap pointed to the prairie's edge and the trees beyond. They climbed out, leaving Holler inside as a precaution.

"You can have a look, but don't get too close, and remember, don't put your fingers in the holes and give that bear a treat," Liz said.

Curtis looked up at Liz and cautiously approached the trap. The bear smelled the boy and grunted and sniffed. Curtis leaned down to get a better look in one of the holes. The bear opened wide, showing his surprisingly short teeth, and growled in Curtis's face. Startled, Curtis waved his hand in front of his face. "Wow, bad breath," He said, backing up. His feet tangled, and he landed on his backside in the dirt.

Seth and Liz tried to hide their smiles as they helped Curtis up.

"That was amazing," Curtis laughed when he got his breath back. "But I expected him to have big, long teeth."

"For one thing, he's young, like a teenager. Black bears don't have long teeth, only less than an inch long. Those teeth are very sharp and can tear you to shreds."

Curtis and Liz stood well behind their truck when Seth was ready to release the bear atop the trap.

Liz gripped a high-powered rifle just in case. Most of the time, the released animal would scramble to the tree line as fast as possible, but there was always one time when things could go horribly wrong.

Seth stood at the back of the trap and released the door in the front. The bear sniffed the air, not moving for several heart-stopping seconds, and then bounded out and into the woods.

Curtis took in a deep breath. He had forgotten to breathe. Seeing the young bear running free into the woods was an unbelievable experience for the young boy. Holler was jumping around in the vehicle, trying to chase after the bear. Even though the dog was in his twilight years, he still had the heart of the hound in him and the will to give chase in his blood.

"Good thing we left him inside," Liz laughed.

"That was so cool," Curtis said. "I can't believe I just saw a real live bear release."

"Curtis, if you work hard and become an FWC officer, you can do this kind of thing every day," Liz said.

"Officer Corday, that's what I want more than anything else in this world."

"Come on, let's get moving. Next stop is the Hillsborough Seminole Reservation in Tampa."

Curtis slid in beside the excited dog and endured all Holler's sniffing and licks. "It's OK, Holler, that bear is long gone now. Settle down. We have more adventure ahead of us. We'll see some real Florida Indians like in my history books."

It wasn't long before Curtis and Holler were asleep in the back seat, and Liz and Seth could talk softly.

"Thanks for letting Curtis come along today," Liz said.

"I like the kid too. He's had a tough go of things. I'm happy to help him out."

"Do you think Latimer will show up here?"

"If he's smart, he'll try and leave the country for a bit," Seth said, glancing at Liz. "Border Patrol will be looking for him and his smuggling network.

"I hope they catch him and whoever is helping him. I've been researching how they ship these turtles. It's horrible how they sometimes tape the turtles in their shells so they can't move. The mortality rate can be as high as thirty-five percent on a shipment, and the traffickers don't give a damn."

Seth held his breath as a car passed them on the double yellow line on a single-lane rural road. "Some people just have a death wish."

Liz was holding on to the door handle so tight her knuckles were white. "But they take others with them. I can't see taking the chance."

"Never mind the idiots. We can stop in Bartow, get something to eat, and let Holler do his thing. We can stay on SR 60. It will take us straight into Tampa. We will be there in plenty of time."

"I just want to be in something that's not moving for a while," Liz said, putting her head back and trying to relax, still gripping the door handle. Even though she did a lot of driving in her job, the stupid things some drivers did still amazed her. Unfortunately, the FWC attended to several traffic fatalities. Some of them involved crashes between deer and cars.

Chapter Sixty-One

The little café in Bartow had a covered outdoor dining area that allowed dogs. Much to the old hound's delight, the waiter gushed over Holler and brought him a big bowl of cold water. They had just started to dig into their hamburgers when Liz's phone buzzed in her pocket.

Liz pulled the phone out and looked at the caller ID, "Damn, what now?" she dropped her burger and put on a pleasant smile.

"Hello, Captain. What can we do for you?"

"Latimer has been spotted at the Miami airport by their security. He was stopped at passport control trying to board a plane for Singapore. Before the Customs and Border inspectors got there, he had disappeared. They're searching for him now. It's a huge area, and he could easily exit the airport, but we are trying to prevent that."

"Any idea who he was working with at the airport?"

"Not yet. We're working on it. Our FWC officers and the Customs Inspectors are there now, checking everyone and the cargo. No one and nothing is going anywhere."

"Thanks for letting us know. We appreciate it." Liz punched off and looked between Seth and Curtis.

Curtis was finished with his lunch. "Hey, why don't you take Holler for a walk around the edge of those trees over there? We still have a while to go, and he could use a good walk before we get back on the road."

"Sure thing, come on, Holler," Curtis said, happy to explore even for a little bit.

Seth watched the boy and dog go and turned to Liz, "Could Latimer possibly return to our area if he can't get out of the country? He is facing jail time here."

"You never know what a desperate man will do," Liz said.

"I hope he stays far away from here and lets Curtis and Dusty have the life they deserve," Seth said, smiling at Curtis and his canine pal exploring the tree line.

Curtis shook his head when he came upon trash blown in from the careless diners. Before moving on, he picked it up and put it in a trash can.

Stepping deeper into the cool shade of the large oak trees, he came to a shallow creek bed. He stopped and sat on the bank with Holler to watch the rippling water. Minnows sparkled in the stream, unaware of his presence. A splash from the other bank father down caught his attention. Several river cooters basked in a patch of sun on a moss-covered log.

"Hey, look, Holler. The bad guys missed some." Curtis chuckled, picked up the dog's leash, and hurried back to tell what he had seen.

Before Curtis returned, Liz said. "I hope they can catch Latimer and put his ass in jail and throw away the key," Liz grumbled.

"I know what you mean. I can't understand how people think it's OK to treat animals like they did."

"Hey, guys," Curtis shouted, running up to Seth and Liz. "there's this stream back there, and you'll never guess what I saw?"

"A pink flamingo," Liz said, laughing.

Curtis looked at her like she was nuts, "No, a whole bunch of river cooters sitting on a log. It was so neat. The bad guys missed them."

"Oh, Curtis, that's wonderful," Liz said. Liz couldn't resist hugging the boy.

Seth picked up their trash. "Let's saddle up. Next stop is the Seminole Rez.

On the road again, Liz felt her phone buzzing away in her

pocket. She answered before looking at the caller ID and immediately regretted it.

"It's my mother," she whispered.

"Hello, Mom. After our last encounter, I didn't think I'd hear from you for a while."

"Things can always change. I was watching the news and saw all about your exploits in capturing some dangerous turtle traffickers. It said two people were killed and that you and your boyfriend rescued two kidnapped boys. I can't believe you are still putting yourself in that situation. Elizabeth, you could have been killed."

Liz wanted to put the phone on speaker for Seth to hear but thought Curtis didn't need to know all her personal history.

"You know that I'm only saying this because I love you. My friends at the club saw the news and asked me about it and your job with the FWC. Frankly, I didn't know what to say."

"Mom, you should be proud that I helped to take some very dangerous people and put them away and save two young boys from getting killed, not to mention over two hundred Florida freshwater turtles from being smuggled to rich people in China." Liz tried to control her temper but found it very hard to keep a lid on it. Her mom was fortunate that Curtis was in the truck. Otherwise, Liz would let Constance Corday have it, swearing and all.

"I do know that, Elizabeth," Constance said, further aggravating Liz by using her formal name.

"I've been talking to an excellent plastic surgeon here in Tallahassee. He's a little older but has an extensive practice, a vacation home in Maine, and a yacht. I'm sure you two would get along famously."

"Mom, if he's such a great catch, why don't you marry him?" Liz had enough and ended the call. "I'm changing my phone number," she said to Seth. Liz wanted to throw her phone out the window. She turned her head to stare out the window watching the scenery whiz past.

"That went well?" Seth said, shaking his head with a slight smile and a query in his eyes.

"She wants me to marry a Tallahassee plastic surgeon. Can you believe it? She saw the news report of what we did and still thinks I want the country club life. The woman is deranged."

"Sweetheart, I don't know what her problem is. All I know is that I love you just the way you are."

"Love you too, Chief."

Seth and Liz couldn't help smiling as they heard quiet snickering from the back seat.

"Dusty would say you two need to get a room. Whatever that means."

Chapter Sixty-Two

"Come on in," Rowena said, greeting Liz and Seth warmly at the door.

"Hi, Mom," Seth replied, hugging her. "Is Dad home?"

"He's out back manning the barbecue grill. Who is this young man with you?"

Curtis stood in the doorway wide-eyed, looking at Seth's mother. Rowena had dressed in the traditional Seminole dress of a floor-length skirt with a colorful ruffled band around the bottom. Her top was like a full cape with a matching ruffled band at the waist and neck. Rowena's black hair was pulled back and knotted close to her head. She was a striking woman with kind eyes and a welcoming smile.

Curtis looked around the home and was surprised to see a regular family home, not the Seminole Indian chickee his schoolbooks showed.

"This is Curtis Dunbar. He was involved with some turtle traffickers we captured. We can tell you all about that later," Seth said, not wanting to upset Curtis.

"Curtis here might like to be an FWC officer one day, and he's very interested in the fact that I'm a Seminole."

"And Curtis, who's your friend there?" Rowena asked.

Curtis looked up at Rowena and down at Holler, "This is Holler. I hope it's OK that I brought him?"

"Of course, come out and meet Seth's Dad." Rowena led the way to the back-screened porch.

Letting Seth and Curtis walk ahead, Rowena linked arms with

Liz. "I'm so happy you came. We have some exciting news to share with both of you."

"I want to talk with you too." Liz confided. "I've had to make some hard decisions lately. You are one person I can count on to help me make another."

Seth's mother thought this decision might include her son's future. In Rowena's mind, Seth and Liz were a perfect match. She could only hope that Liz saw it that way, too.

Liz stepped onto the porch and saw Seth's father talking with Curtis. Andres Grayson was old-school Seminole. He didn't show his emotions often but smiled broadly at Curtis's stories about his adventures with Holler.

"Hi, Liz," Andres called. "Your young man here is quite the adventurer. He was telling me about finding a dead body in the woods." The older man's eyes had a question in them.

"Yes, we had some trouble with turtle traffickers, and they murdered one of their own and left the body in the woods. Curtis and his friend Dusty came across it and reported it to the FWC because it was on state land."

Andres returned to the grill to check on the chicken and the corn roasting away. The smoky smell was drifting in, making everyone hungry.

"You will have to tell us more about that. We have some news for you as well."

Seth looked at his mom, fearing the worst, like a medical condition he didn't want to hear about.

"It's nothing bad," Rowena said, realizing how Seth might be jumping to the wrong conclusion.

"We're moving!" Andres said with a huff. "The reservation here is not like in the old days. The casino and hotel have taken over, and there is no place for the people to live. The old sandlot where you and your friends played ball is now a car park. Your mom and I have to go to Tampa for medical treatment. The casino has swallowed up all the neighborhood facilities we had while you were growing up."

"Where are you moving to?" Seth asked, his eyebrows lifting.

"I think you will be happy with our decision. We will talk more later. Now we will eat."

Liz went to help Rowena set the table and left the men to talk. Curtis found an old ball and tossed it to Holler until the dog gave up and saw a soft spot to relax. The dog was getting on in years, almost as old as his master, and finding it hard to keep up with a thirteen-year-old boy.

During dinner, Curtis asked Seth and his parents about life growing up as a Seminole. He was fascinated and so curious in a good way. Curtis also wanted to know more about being an FWC office and their job. Before long, it was time to go to the small community center for the dance.

As they walked into the center, Seth again felt all eyes on him and Liz from people they knew. This time the added question was, who was the young boy with them?

Rowena and Andres found seats with their friends George and Mina Reynolds and introduced Curtis as a friend of theirs.

Discovering Curtis's interest in their culture, everyone at their table was happy to talk about the old days and how the casino had changed things.

"This is what I was talking to Seth about," Andres said. "Rowena and I are moving to Big Cypress Rez. There is nothing here for us anymore. We have had relatives asking us to move down there for several years, and we will finally do it. I have family down there, and Seth has cousins. Row and I have been thinking about it for a while now."

George looked at Mina. Mina smiled broadly and nodded at George.

Seeing the exchange, Rowena asked, "OK, what's going on?"

"We didn't want to say anything, but we are moving too," George said. "You are right about the casino. It's not the same as in the old days."

Mina reached out to take Rowena's hand. "But if you're moving too, it won't be so bad because…. We are moving to Big Cypress too, and I can't wait. Maybe we can even be neighbors."

The men shook their heads in agreement as the women hugged. It was all going to work out. Friends and neighbors would find a new life living the old life they knew.

The music started, and Seth took Liz onto the floor to dance Seminole traditional step dances. Liz was getting good at following the rhythm of the drums and the beat of the steps as the dancers flowed.

The next dance was the Alligator Dance. A traditional dance and the first dance that Liz had learned. As Seth and Liz danced, they saw Rowena leading a nervous Curtis through the steps. By the third time around the floor, Curtis was leading and smiling from ear to ear.

Back at the table, an exhausted Curtis tried hard to cover up a wide yawn.

"Sorry folks, we were up early, and I think our young friend here has had enough excitement for one night," Seth said.

"Yes, I can see that," Rowena said, smiling and ruffling Curtis's hair. "We'll walk back with you."

Seth and his dad walked with Curtis while Liz and Rowena strolled a little behind.

"Can I ask you something?" Liz said. "My mom is no help with stuff like this. She wants me to move to Tallahassee, marry a plastic surgeon, and join her country club."

"And I'm thinking that's not what you want?

"No, it's not. I'm happy with Seth and my life with him and my work with the FWC."

"So, what's the question?" Rowena knew what was coming and walked slower and farther behind the men.

"How do you know when it's the right time to get married? I mean, it's supposed to be for life, till death do you part and all that stuff. I know Seth would like to be married, and I think I want to marry him, but I'm afraid I'll mess it up."

Rowena looked at Liz and stopped her. "Do you love Seth?

"With all my heart."

"Then everything will be as it should be. Don't let your mother's mistakes influence you because you are not your mother. We have talked a bit about your mother and father and how you miss your father. She tried to change your father into what she wanted him to be. Seth loves you for who you are, and you love him the same way. You are on the same path in life. Share it and enjoy it."

Liz tilted her head and looked at Rowena. "You know you're right."

"Then quit torturing me and give me some grandbabies to spoil."

Chapter Sixty-Three

Curtis was sleeping when they stopped in front of his house just before midnight. The porch light immediately flicked on, casting a slight glow over the yard. Curtis's parents greeted Seth and Liz. The parents had been up waiting and talking. The events of the past few days, as horrible as they were, had brought them together again.

Looking in the back seat of Seth's truck, a smile crossed Lorraine's face as she saw her son fast asleep with his dog across his lap. "I almost hate to wake him."

"I'll get him," Bob Dunbar said, opening the door and rousing the dog first. Holler looked up with sad, sleepy eyes and rolled off onto his feet and out of the door to the nearest tree. It took a couple shakes to get a response out of Curtis.

"Hi, Dad. Are we home already?"

Bob Dunbar smiled at his sleepy son, "Yes, you're home. Come on. Let's get you to bed."

"I met real Indians today. It was so cool. I even danced with them," A very sleepy Curtis mumbled.

"Thanks, I had a great time today," Curtis said to Liz and Seth, stifling a huge yawn.

Eventually, the boy was up and moving up the steps to his bed, guided by his dad.

"Thank you so much for all you have done for Curtis and us," Lorraine Dunbar said.

"We enjoyed having Curtis with us today," Seth said.

"I mean with my father and the turtles and all. I don't know what I would have done if anything had happened to Curtis."

"We are not out of the woods yet. Keep Curtis close to home for a while, or have someone with him and Dusty. I'll be in touch. It should all be over soon." Liz tried to be confident, but until Latimer was caught, or they were sure he had fled the country, Curtis and Dusty could still be in danger.

Watching the little house in the rearview mirror, Seth saw Mr. and Mrs. Dunbar wave and walk hand and hand into the house. *Maybe something good did come out of this mess after all.*

He reached across the seat and took Liz's hand, rubbing his thumb over her knuckles. Her head was against the headrest with her eyes closed. "We did a good thing today. Curtis will remember today for the rest of his life. By the way, I talked with your mother."

Seth looked sideways at Liz. "Is that a good thing or a bad thing?" he said. Liz was closer to his mother than she was to her own and would be able to share feelings she couldn't otherwise.

"I think it's a good thing."

They drove the rest of the way to Sarasota in silence. All the time, Seth was wondering what Liz and his mother had talked about. The only thing he could be sure of was that his mother would offer advice from her heart.

Chapter Sixty-Four

A note from their dog sitter and friend, Darrell, waited for them on the table when they got home.

> *Hi folks,*
>
> *You might want to know that there is a skunk prowling around out back. Nokosi almost had a run-in with him, but Marcia spotted the skunk early this evening, just as we were about to let Nokosi out for the last time before we took off.*
>
> *I'll drop a trap off on my way to work in the morning. Give me a call when you have the critter, and I'll set him loose somewhere in the park where he won't stink up the place.*
>
> *Darrell*

Seth sat at the table and laughed. "We trapped and released a bear. Now we get home and have to trap a skunk. I don't know which smells worse?"

Liz came up behind him and rested her chin on his head. "I think you might have a tie there. That bear was pretty rank, but I don't think any grocery store would stock enough tomato juice to take the skunk smell off Nokosi if he tangled with one. I don't even want to think about it."

Seth pulled Liz onto his lap and began to explore her neck with his lips. "Hmm, you taste salty."

"I need a shower," Liz said. "You don't smell like any bed of roses either, Chief." She pushed off and took his hand, "Come on. I know the way."

Damp from their shower, Seth and Liz cuddled on the couch, watching a Hallmark movie they had seen a dozen times before.

"Remember I said I was talking to your mother," Liz said, taking a deep breath and biting her lower lip. She knew what she wanted to say and needed to summon up the courage to find the right words.

Seth knew something had been weighing on her since they left his parent's house. He patiently waited for her to continue.

"Well, you know how much I love you and want to be with you, but I'm afraid I'll mess up the happily ever after thing."

"It's OK, sweetheart," Seth whispered, kissing the top of her head as she rested against his chest."

"I was thinking…."

"Yes."

"What do you think about a long engagement?"

Seth gently pushed Liz up so he could look into her eyes. "Are you serious?"

Liz was afraid he was upset, and a tear leaked from the corner of her eye and rolled down her cheek.

Seth caught it with a kiss, "I think that is a terrific idea. Do I get to put a ring on your finger?"

Liz looked up, a slight smile on her lips as she nodded yes.

Chapter Sixty-Five

The sun was barely up, streaking the sky with shades of flamingo pink and magenta tinged with brilliant gold.

Seth rocked on the front porch watching Nokosi sniff around. He watched the dog closely as the smell of skunk lingered faintly on the breeze. Darrell would drop off the live trap this morning, and he could relocate his unwanted visitor to a more welcoming place in Manasota State Park.

Liz came out holding two mugs of coffee. She handed one to Seth and sat in the rocker beside him. "It's lovely this time of day."

"Another hour, and it will be getting too hot to enjoy. What are your plans for the day?"

"I'm checking out boat ramps, the usual stuff, and if they have the boats registered, life preservers, fire extinguishers, fishing licenses while I'm at it. What are you going to get up to?"

"I've got an itch that needs scratching. I'm going to follow up with Captain Jacobs about Jarod Henderson and Maxwell Latimer. So far as I know, Latimer is still out there, and that worries me."

Seth called Nokosi in and helped Liz up from her chair. They cleared up the few dishes and dressed for the day ahead.

Seth's phone rang as he closed the door and headed to his truck. Liz was inside, fussing with her uniform and finishing getting ready.

When Liz came out, Seth was sitting on the porch steps.

"What's up, Chief? You're wearing that worried face again,"

Liz said, sitting beside him.

"Captain Jacobs called. They lost track of Latimer at the Miami airport. They can only suspect that he is still in this country."

Liz sat beside him and leaned against Seth. "That's not good. I'd be happier knowing for sure where he is. What about Jarod Henderson? Is he still in custody?"

"So far. Let's hope he stays there. What I'm worried about Dusty and Curtis? If Latimer ever gets caught, the boys are prime witnesses, and their testimony would convict both Henderson and Latimer of multiple charges. What if he tries to silence them? Witnesses do get killed, so they can't testify."

It won't be over until Latimer and Henderson are both behind bars," Liz said, taking one last sip of her cold coffee. Any boaters would be launching soon, and she needed to be there when they did.

Seth pushed up from the step and looked at a flock of egrets flying from their night roost. "I'll wander over to Manasota Park and take Nokosi with me. He hasn't had a decent walk in a while. I can check in with Darrell, maybe save him the trouble of dropping the trap off."

"You could always check fishing licenses with me if you want," Liz suggested.

"Sorry, sweetheart, I love you, but I don't want to be cooped up in a vehicle today."

Seth reached out to help her off her seat on the porch step. Once on her feet, he encircled her in his arms and held her tight. "Question. Do I tell Darrell we are engaged? Or wait until we can show off a shiny ring on your finger?

"Let's wait and have Darrell and Marcia over for a meal and tell them then. That would be fun."

"What about my parents and your mother?"

"Your mother will be over the moon. Mine, not so much. Let's wait until I have that ten-carat diamond on my finger, and we can go visit them wherever they are."

"Ten carats, really? You do realize I work for the FWC?"

"I'm open to negotiations."

Chapter Sixty-Six

A late model Honda with stolen plates sat idling by the curb down the block from Curtis Dunbar's house.

Max Latimer sat behind the wheel, watching Curtis and Dusty on the porch steps.

Latimer had been unsuccessful in finding a plane to take him out of the country in Miami. The security at check-in had prevented him. The first time he presented his passport for an international flight, it raised a red flag. He barely escaped by using a ruse to lure a janitor off the concourse and take his uniform. With that as a disguise, he fled the airport.

He figured his best course of action was to eliminate anyone who could testify against him.

He stole a car from the long-term parking lot late yesterday and driven to Nocatee in Desoto County using the back roads.

Once Latimer stole the car, he stopped in Naples and swapped the Honda plates on the stolen car for plates from another Honda he found parked at a strip mall. Latimer felt proud of himself and thought he had outsmarted all the cops and security running around the airport looking for him.

Latimer continued to watch the boys and think about how to silence them.

"Yeah, that Jarod guy is in jail, but the other one, Latimer, is a real badass. So, we gotta stay put." Dusty looked at what Curtis was doing and shook his head. He knew his cousin was bored, but there was not much they could do about it.

Latimer took out a burner phone and made a phone call. It took a few minutes, but he accomplished the first part of his plan easily.

Leaving the boys, he drove to Arcadia and waited across the street from the DeSoto County Jail, where Jarod Henderson was awaiting transfer to state custody.

Latimer's phone vibrated in his pocket. Smiling, he recognized the number and answered.

"Did they accept it?" Latimer asked.

"Yeah., He should be walking through the doors any minute."

Latimer hung up. Getting out of the car, he threw the phone on the ground and stomped, and tossed it into a waste bin.

A half hour later, Henderson walked out the doors of the county jail.

Jarod stood on the steps, his eyes adjusting to the bright sun. He was shocked to find Latimer standing beside him. He was even more surprised by the gun poking into his ribs.

"You're probably wondering who posted your bail?" Latimer said. "You cost me a pretty penny, but as I said before, I don't like to leave any loose ends, and you, my friend, are a loose end."

Jarod wished he was back in his comfy cell. "What do you want from me?"

"You're going to help me with those two pesky kids." Latimer poked the gun into Jarod's ribs harder.

"What are you going to do to them?" Jarod had a pretty good idea and didn't like it.

"I'm not going to do anything to them. I thought the boys might like going on a little fishing trip. Young boys like that have to be so careful out on the water alone. Don't you agree?"

Chapter Sixty-Seven

"I don't see why we can't go out and do stuff," Curtis said. He was bored. He wanted to get back out into the woods exploring or fishing on the Peace, anything. Or he would go crazy.

"We have to wait until they catch that Latimer guy," Dusty answered. Dusty was OK with staying close to home. He could read a book or be happy with a board game.

"What about that other one, Jarod somebody? He's in jail, right?" Curtis absently played with a small ant, putting sticks and pebbles for obstacles. "What if they don't catch Latimer, and he comes back for us?"

"Let's not go borrowing trouble. You want to help me make some Kool-Aid?"

"Nah, I want to see how long it takes this ant to figure out how to get around all this stuff I put in his way."

Dusty went inside, leaving Curtis to play in the dirt with his sticks, rocks, and ants.

Bob and Lorraine Dunbar had left the cousins alone at their house while shopping for clothes for her new job at the bank. It was so long since she had new clothes Lorraine was not even sure of her size anymore. The nearest Walmart was in Arcadia, twenty minutes away.

Dusty brought out two ice-filled glasses of raspberry Kool-Aid and sat down beside Curtis and holler.

A dust-covered Honda pulled up to the curb. Curtis and Dusty watched wide-eyed in terror. Max Latimer and Jarod Henderson ran toward them.

"Aw, we're not going to hurt you. The cops let us go." Latimer lied. "We were thinking about how badly we treated you and want to make up for it."

Latimer could turn on the charm when he wanted. Jarod rolled his eyes at the line of bull. Jarod also knew that Latimer had a gun tucked in his belt under his shirt and would not hesitate to use it on him or the boys.

"What say we take a little fishing trip on the river? You two must know of a boat we could use. I bet you haven't been fishing in a while."

"We can't leave the house without a parent," Dusty said, standing up. He didn't trust Latimer. Something was wrong. The sheriff would not just let these men out of jail without telling anyone. Surely Officer Grayson or Officer Corday would have let them know.

"I want to go fishing, Dusty, but my mom said to stay home," Curtis pleaded. "What should we do?" Curtis was afraid of Latimer but so wanted to do anything but sit at home all day. He couldn't see the harm of a little fishing trip. Curtis figured they could be back before his parents came home, and they wouldn't have to know. Curtis didn't always see the danger in things the way Dusty did.

Dusty figured it could go very bad, very quickly, if they didn't go with the men. He had to think fast.

"Let me call my dad and tell him we are going fishing. I don't want him to worry." Dusty said, stalling for time.

He wanted to call Officer Corday for help. He was fingering another one of the officer's cards with her number deep in his pocket. Liz had insisted he keep couple in his pockets after the incident with the ranger.

"Curtis's mom and dad are out shopping, but my folks sometimes come home for lunch. If we're not here, they might call the cops."

The last thing Latimer wanted was for the sheriff or the pesky FWC officers to come nosing around. "Go ahead but make it quick."

"Here, use my phone," Latimer said, pushing his burner phone into Dusty's hands.

"I have my dad's new work number written down," Dusty said, pulling a scrap of card.

Dusty prayed Officer Corday would answer and understand what he was trying to tell her.

Panic set in as Dusty waited for the phone to ring.

"Yeah, hi, Dad. This is Dusty. Sorry to bother you at work. Two old friends came by and are taking us fishing on the river."

"That's right."

"We are going to use the old johnboat like we did before. You know when Gramps told us about monkey fishing."

"Yeah, that's the place."

"Curtis and I wanted you to know so you wouldn't worry."

Dusty listened for a moment and then hung up.

Dusty took a breath. Liz had understood and told him to play along. She'd contact Seth and the sheriff. Liz told Dusty not to worry. Her stomach was rolling, frightened at what might happen.

Mrs. Chavez saw two men she didn't know talking to Curtis and Dusty from her window. She had a bad feeling that something was not right.

Opening her front door, she called out to the boys, "Curtis, Dusty is everything alright?"

Dusty saw Latimer reaching for the gun in his belt. "We're fine, Mrs. Chavez. I called to let Dad know we're going fishing. Can you take care of Holler for us? We're going on the Peace, and he don't like boats. You can call him to be sure if you want."

Mrs. Chavez was in her late seventies but knew there was a subtext message in there somewhere. She had numbers for Officers Corday and Grayson and the Desoto County Sheriff.

It took several minutes to dig in her kitchen drawer to find the number she was looking for. Her hands were shaking as she held the phone and punched in Seth's number.

"Officer Grayson, I'm so glad I got you. Something terrible happened. I just saw two men talking to Dusty and Curtis outside.

I asked them if they were OK, and Dusty said they were going fishing with these men. I know they were not supposed to go anywhere without their parents. Then I saw these men take the boys. I'm so afraid they've been kidnapped again. Dusty told me to call his dad to check that it was OK for them to go fishing and for me to watch Holler because the dog doesn't like boats. It was all so strange."

"Thanks, Mrs. Chavez. Officer Corday called me because Dusty called and got a message to her as well. This all helps. We're on our way. We'll bring them back safely. We know where they have gone, thanks to Dusty. He's one smart kid."

Chapter Sixty-Eight

He'd enjoyed the walk with Nokosi and the time to clear his head, but now all he wanted to do was get back with Liz to save Dusty and Curtis.

Seth was glad he didn't have to hike back to the trailhead from Gator Hollow as he heard the rumbling of Darrell's four-wheeler. It was a long two-mile hike through the pristine dry Florida prairie to Gator Hollow, where alligators gathered in their hundreds in a deep sinkhole created hundreds of years ago along the side of the Myakka River.

He could only imagine that Latimer had made his way back from Miami. The lives of anyone that might be able to testify against Latimer were in danger.

Pulling to a stop beside Seth, Darrell shouted, "Hey, Chief, need a ride?" His lopsided grin always made Seth laugh but not this morning.

"Yeah, Liz just told me those two boys, Curtis and Dusty, have been abducted again. One of them got a message to her."

Seth talked as he climbed up behind Darrell and somehow got Nokosi on his lap.

"Chief, you need a smaller dog." The engine roared as they raced back to the trailhead.

Jumping into his truck, Seth called Liz. "Hi, I'm on my way. I got a call from Mrs. Chavez. She saw the two men with Dusty and

Curtis. Dusty gave her the same message he gave you but said they were going fishing on the Peace. I think they are going to where I first met them. You know it? I'll meet you there. I'll call the Sheriff, and you can call Jacobs. We need to get a few more boots on the ground there."

"I'm in the Duette Nature Preserve in Manatee County." Liz said. "It's primitive out here, but I'll get there as quickly as possible. Like I said this morning, I was going to check fishing licenses, and I haven't been out here in a while. People tend to get lazy if the FWC doesn't show up once in a while."

Liz still had her job to do and had been hoping that Latimer was on his way out of the area.

"When we get Curtis back, I'd like to bring him out here. This is how Florida used to look before all the developers moved in. He'd love it here."

"Good idea. I'll see you soon," Seth said, starting his truck and throwing the A/C on high. Once again, he had Darrell to thank for taking care of Nokosi in an emergency.

"Before you go," Liz said, stopping Seth. "I talked to the DeSoto County Sheriff. Jarod Henderson was bailed out."

"How the hell did that happen? When did it happen?"

"Somebody came up with the money. I'm willing to bet it was somebody Latimer is working for. It was something like half a million, maybe more. Somebody sure doesn't want Henderson talking. The officer I spoke with didn't know who. He said he would look into it. I'm not going to hold my breath."

"See you up there," Seth said, hanging up. He was heading east on SR 72 to Arcadia to catch US17 to Zolfo Springs. He first met the boys when he saw them monkey fishing on the Peace River. That had to be where they were heading.

He had three lives to save now, Dusty, Curtis, and now Jarod Henderson.

Chapter Sixty-Nine

Latimer was driving and shouting into the hands-free phone at the same time. "Tell Mr. Chang I understand we have an agreement.

Tell him I am very sorry for the death of his daughter. It was a tragic accident."

The person on the other end was yelling so loudly Latimer had to turn down the volumn.

"No, it is not necessary to send anyone to assist me."

Another blast from the other end followed.

Softening his tone, Latimer continued, "I have some cleaning up to do here, and then we can move the operation to another area. I am sure I can secure a team to collect more turtles for Mr. Chang's enterprise shortly. There is no need to send anyone."

The person on the other end barked some orders that had Latimer shaking his head and swearing under his breath.

"Yes, I will expect him. Send me the information."

Latimer hit the button on the steering wheel to disconnect the call. "Shit, that's all I need. At least I don't have to deal with Chang's maniac daughter anymore."

Jarod was sitting in the passenger seat, smirking that Latimer was in trouble with his boss.

Latimer scowled back and made a sharp turn into Pioneer Park in Zolfo Springs.

"OK, boys, where's the boat ramp and this boat of yours?"

"How we gonna go fishing? We don't have our poles or any bait." Curtis said. It had finally dawned on him that something wasn't right. Dusty silently nudged him to shut up. That's when Curtis grew afraid. Tears glistened in Curtis's eyes.

Dusty spoke up and told Latimer to follow the road to the left. It was the long way around to the boat ramp. He prayed that Officer Corday understood what he was trying to tell her. Mrs. Chavez had seen the men take them. Maybe she called for help too.

The boat ramp was deserted in the early afternoon. Most people avoided the afternoon heat and would come out later when it cooled down.

The old boat was just where the cousins had left it weeks ago. It was tied up to a pine tree a few yards downstream from the ramp.

"Jarod, help the boys get the boat ready." Latimer barked.

Latimer spotted a gator on the opposite bank. The creature could play into his plan very nicely.

"Where are the fishing poles?" Curtis asked again. "We can't go fishing without poles and bait."

"I have them in the trunk of the car. Get in the boat, and I'll get them." Latimer saw Dusty hesitate.

Jarod knew there were no fishing rods in the back of the car. He didn't trust Latimer and tried to think of a way to save the boys and himself. Latimer meant to kill the boys and possibly him as well. He just had to look for the right moment.

"No, I don't want to go," Curtis said, beginning to cry.

Latimer shoved him. "You will if you know what's good for you." Brandishing the gun at the boys.

"Come on, we don't have a choice," Dusty whispered to his cousin.

Dusty and Curtis climbed in the boat, and Latimer pushed them away from the dock.

Suddenly Latimer picked up a paddle left beside a kayak and tried to tip the boat over.

"Hey, what are you doing?" Curtis cried.

Water sloshed over the side of the hull. The boat was in danger of being swamped when Jarod tore the paddle from Latimer's hands.

Jarod raised the paddle to hit Latimer. A shot rang out through the silence, and he felt the hot, sharp pain of a bullet piercing his midsection. He dropped the paddle, collapsing on the rough wooden planks of the boat ramp.

"One problem solved," Latimer said as he dragged Jarod to the edge of the ramp and rolled him into the water. A dark red stain eddied down the river.

"Lunch is served," Latimer called to the gator across the river.

The splash attracted the alligator, and Dusty and Curtis watched in horror as the reptile silently slid down the bank and slipped under the surface. Their boat was slowly sinking, and Jarod was floating face down a few feet away from them.

Latimer looked pleased with his handiwork as another gator slid into the amber water. A flash of reflective light in the trees on the opposite bank caught his attention.

"Shit, sorry, fellas, gotta go," Latimer said as he ran for his car.

Latimer had spotted a DeSoto sheriff's vehicle and knew more were on the way. He had to get out of the park before the roads were closed down and his escape impossible. Not knowing the roads, he took the same road out and somehow managed to miss Seth and Liz converging on the boat ramp.

Liz and Seth jumped out of their vehicles and ran to the river bank, calling for Dusty and Curtis.

"Help Jarod," Dusty yelled, trying to help Curtis swim for the bank. "He tried to save us. Latimer shot him."

The cousins were scrambling up the bank. Liz reached out to give them a hand. Dusty and Curtis made it just as an alligator snapped at their heels.

The bull gator had his sights on the wounded man floating, unconscious, and oozing blood into the slow-moving water—a red trail of blood flowing downstream.

Seth jumped in, grabbing Jarod around the shoulders, hauling the big man towards the bank. They got the unconscious man on shore seconds before the huge reptile would have dragged him under to make a meal of him.

Feeling for a pulse and finding none, Liz began CPR with Seth assisting. After a frantic few minute, Jarod came back and started to breathe again, spitting up river water and blood.

"Dusty, get the first aid box out of my truck, quick. We have to stop the bleeding," Liz said.

"Curtis, take my phone. The sheriff's number is in there. Put it on speaker when you get them," Seth said.

"I've never used one before," Curtis mumbled.

"You're smarter than you know. You can do it."

Curtis fumbled a bit, but finally, he had the sheriff on the line.

"Latimer got away. He shot Jared Henderson, and we need an ambulance here fast. He tried to kill Dusty and me." Curtis said.

Dusty returned with the first aid box. Liz and Seth went to work helping to keep Jared stabilized.

The ambulance took fifteen minutes to arrive, but it seemed like hours. The EMS techs did their best and bundled Jarod up for the trip to DeSoto Memorial in Arcadia.

Sitting on the ground, Seth and Liz looked at the boys.

"Care to explain what part of *don't leave the house without a parent* you didn't understand?" Seth was upset that the boys had put themselves in a risky position to be hurt. He was also proud of Dusty for getting a message to Liz that they were in trouble.

Liz was on the phone to Captain Jacobs about Latimer being on the loose in area. He would coordinate with the sheriff's office to try and track him down again.

Liz walked slowly down the riverbank with Seth.

"You got something on your mind chief?"

"Just thinking about what could have happened."

He also wondered if this was what being a parent was like, loving your kids so much and being so afraid at the same time? Was he ready for that?

Chapter Seventy

"Let's get you home," Seth said, wrapping each of the boys in a silver survival blanket.

"We're sorry, but we had to go with them," Dusty said after several minutes.

Liz turned in her seat to look at Dusty. "It's OK. Tell us what happened."

"They came up to the house and said the police let them go. I kinda knew that wasn't right. Then the Latimer guy says he wants to take us fishing."

Curtis started to cry again. "I wanted to go. It's all my fault. I was so bored staying at the house all the time."

"It wasn't your fault, Curtis. Latimer had a gun. I saw it under his shirt. He might have shot us right there." Dusty said hugging his cousin.

"We had to go. Curtis's mom and dad were shopping but might come home and be shot too. I made up how I had to call my dad at work. I called you instead," Dusty said, looking at Officer Corday. "I had your extra cards in my pocket and hoped you understood my message."

"You did great. Mrs. Chavez called Officer Grayson, and we figured out the rest."

"Jarod tried to save us. Latimer tried to tip the boat so the gators would get us. He fought for us, and Latimer shot him and pushed him into the river. That big gator was headed straight for Jarod when you pulled him out."

"Is Jarod going to be alright?" Curtis asked.

"I don't know, but I'll check with the hospital. First, we take you home."

It was a short drive to the Dunbar home. The two cousins were silent in the back seat, afraid of what their parents would say and their punishment.

A sheriff's patrol car and the boy's parents waited in the drive.

Officer Perez from Hardee County stepped over to meet them as they parked.

"Mrs. Chavez filled us in on what happened. She said two men took the boys, but Dusty managed to send her a coded message. She's a pretty smart old lady. She helped us find those kids and got you there in time to save them."

"Dusty got a message to me, too," Liz said. We needed that to get the deputies involved and headed to the river.

"I hope Jarod Henderson pulls through so he can tell us more about Latimer and what he might be planning," Perez said.

Seth and Liz let the boys out of the vehicle. The parents quickly took their sons, the mothers hugging them fiercely. The parents were thankful to have them back in one piece.

"Mom, Dad, I'm so sorry. I just wanted to go fishing," Curtis said. He hugged his mom and looked up cautiously at his dad.

"I'm sorry, Curtis. I should have been around more and taken you fishing. I know how much you like to be out exploring. I'll try to do better." Bob Dunbar had done a lot of thinking the past few days and realized how close he came to losing his family.

Holler wiggled between Lorraine and Curtis, raining sloppy kisses on Curtis.

Curtis sat on the ground with his arms around the dog. "Yeah, I know I was stupid. But now Dad said he's going to take us fishing. Won't that be great? Maybe we can show him the best spots."

Dusty distanced himself from his parents and approached Seth and Liz, who were standing talking with Officer Perez. A map of the area was spread out over the hood of the sheriff's car.

"Officers," Dusty said, interrupting. "I don't know if this will help, but Latimer was talking to someone on the phone while we were going to the park."

"Do you know who he was talking to?" Seth asked.

"No, but they were both yelling and mad. Latimer said to tell Mr. Chang he was sorry about his daughter and that it was an accident. Latimer was mad. Something about Mr. Chang was sending him an assistant. They are going to start collecting turtles again in a different area. Latimer has to meet this assistant. Does that help?"

Officer Perez reached out to Dusty. "You did great. I'd like you to consider joining the force when you get older. You have the mind of a great police officer."

Dusty beamed with pride. Being part of the sheriff's department would be a dream come true.

"You need to finish high school, and a few college courses couldn't hurt either. You get good grades, and maybe we can find a couple scholarships for you."

"Thanks, Officer Perez," Dusty said. He joined his parents to tell them.

"Looks like things are under control here, Captain Jacobs will keep us posted on Latimer. Liz and I will take off." Seth said, shaking hands with the sheriff.

Seth helped Liz into her vehicle, stealing a kiss as she buckled in. "I'll see you at home."

Turning back to his truck, he bumped into Mrs. Chavez, holding a plate of empanadas. "I made these while waiting on word about the boys. I know, some people think I'm just a nosy old widow lady with nothing to do. But I love those boys."

"I can tell Mrs. Chavez," Seth said.

"I have watched over them and Lorraine for years. My own family is grown and moved away. Lorraine needed me as much as I needed her. I hope you understand."

"They are lucky to have a friend like you. Thanks for these. Liz and I will enjoy them tonight."

Chapter Seventy-One

There was one empanada left on the plate.

"You have it," Seth said, being the gentleman.

"No, you take it. I'm stuffed," Liz said, leaning back in her chair.

Seth grabbed the tasty pastry before she could change her mind. "These are really good, better than what you get in the store."

"I won't be able to get my pants on tomorrow."

"I have a great exercise to help you lose a few calories. And you won't even need pants for it," Seth said with a nod to the bedroom.

"Later, Chief. Remember what Dusty said about Latimer meeting someone, an assistant maybe?"

"Yeah, that did concern me. It means that this is not over, and the traffickers will just set up shop somewhere else. I'll call Captain Jacobs. Whoever this Mr. Chang is, he's running this from Singapore."

Liz cleared the few dishes they used and turned from the sink. "It sounds like Latimer was Chang's connection here in Florida. They were in Lee County and moved up here when it got too hot down there. The FWC was closing in and had already rounded up some of them. Meiling was Chang's daughter, and Chang used her as his enforcer to keep Latimer in line and secure the shipment of the turtles. That all fell apart. Chang's organization can't be too happy with Latimer right now."

The puzzle pieces were starting to come together. It was only a matter of time before all the pieces came together.

"Latimer is meeting someone sent by Chang. That person would be landing in Miami from Singapore since that is where the turtles were going to be leaving from. The traffickers have a connection, most likely in the outbound cargo area. Someone must be on Chang's pay- roll. Captain Jacobs can alert airport security and border inspectors to watch for Latimer and whoever he is meeting. I'll call Jacobs."

"You think you'd like a trip down to Miami?"

"That's a little out of our territory, isn't it?" Liz asked.

"Not if we get permission for a special detail to the Miami airport. What do you say?"

"I say, call Captain Jacobs. He will have to run it up the chain of command. The crime was committed in our area, so we have a vested interest. It's our case."

"But remember different agencies don't always play nice together. When it's approved. If it's approved," Seth said. "I can call Darrell to watch Nokosi, and we are on our way to Miami."

Chapter Seventy-Two

Seth walked into the bedroom after talking with Jacobs. He was able to get permission for Seth and Liz to go to Miami and was processing the paperwork. Jacobs did receive warnings about conflicting agencies involved but was able to stress the point that three murders and kidnapping had all occurred in their territory and the prime suspect was on the run.

Liz had two suitcases, and a duffle bag laid out on the bed. She pulled two nice dresses out of the closet.

"Which one should I take?"

Seth thought only a woman would pack this much for a two-day trip. But then again, he did like to see her dress up for date night.

"Take both," he smiled. "You never know. Besides, I had an idea. When this is over, we can stop at Big Cypress and show my parents your big shiny ring."

"Ah, one problem. I don't have that big shiny ring yet."

"Maybe we can get one at the airport gift shop." Seth laughed. He ducked when Liz threw one of her boots at him.

"Oh no, you don't. There are some nice jewelry shops in Coconut Grove."

"Yes, sweetheart. You can have whatever your little heart desires." Seth said, grabbing Liz, taking her down on the bed with him, and pushing the suitcases to the floor.

"Did you remember to call Darrell?" Liz asked, snuggling

deeper into his arms.

"Yes, I did. I told him I owed him and Marcia a big steak dinner as soon as we returned. Darrell said he would take us up on that. Marcia is due to have the baby in another month or so. You could show off the big shiny ring and give them the big news."

"I like that plan. When do we leave?"

"As soon as I fix that flat tire on my truck."

"What flat tire?" Liz asked, and suddenly eyes wide, she smiled. "Oh, that flat tire."

Chapter Seventy-Three

The trip south and across Alligator Alley took five hours. Even though they were leaping into the hunt for a dangerous killer, Liz let her mind wander as she watched the scenery pass. Seth was a great tour guide, explaining how the Tamiami Trail cut through the Everglades and the politics behind its creation. One side of US 41 was dry, cultivated for crops like sugar cane and tomatoes, and developed for housing. The other side had an eight-foot-high chain-link fence topped with barbed wire slanted towards the Everglades. It was not designed to keep people out but to keep animals in. Alligators or deer crossing the highway caused accidents, sometimes fatal. Seth and Liz learned that alligators could climb a chain-link fence while working on the alligator egg poaching case together. Some creatures had learned to use the wildlife tunnels beneath the roadway which helped to protect them.

Heading to Miami, the river of grass was on the right and stretched as far as they could see with the occasional hummock of trees.

"There's a sign for an airboat ride in the Everglades. Can we do that, please, while we're here?" Liz said.

"Catching Max Latimer comes first. I don't want that deranged killer to escape again. We also have to stop whoever he is supposed to be meeting."

"Of course, you're right. I've just never been to this part of Florida before."

"One of my uncles will take us out if we have time. If not, we can always come back. My parents would love to have us visit as much as possible.”

“Do your parents know why we are going to Miami?” Liz asked.

“I only told them it was for work. I didn’t want my mom to worry. If she knew we were after a murderer she would drive my dad crazy with questions about our safety. I love my mom, but she would be calling and checking on us every two minutes. After this is over, we can plan to take a week off and bring Nokosi with us. How does that sound?”

“That sounds wonderful. Maybe I can pick up some brochures for when we come back.”

“You don’t need brochures, sweetheart. We have my family. They have been exploring and hunting in the Everglades for over a hundred years. They are the best tour guides you could ever have.”

Liz saw another sign and wanted to stop at a Seminole souvenir shop. It was decorated to entice tourists on their way to and from Miami. Colorful blankets and woven straw hats hung like banners waving in the wind.

“Another time sweetheart. We have to catch the bad guys first remember them?”

“Sorry I’m bored stuck in the truck for so long. Now I know how Curtis felt stuck in the house and wanting to go fishing.”

“Yeah and look how that almost ended up.” Seth said. He was tired of driving too but the sooner they captured Latimer and put him behind bars the better.

Seth encouraged Liz to wait. “You will love the Museum on the Rez. The name of the museum is Ah-Tah-Thi-Ki. It means a place to learn, a place to remember.”

“You heard from your mom and dad then?”

“They should be there tomorrow. My Uncle Zackery and a couple cousins are helping them unload and set up. By the time we get there, we should be in time for a big barbecue. Uncle Max is out there hunting now.”

“You mean hunting for a parking space at the grocery store, right?”

"Sweetheart, we should have a nice pig roast, fresh fish, and maybe some tasty barbecue alligator. Remember that Seminole Gold barbecue sauce that my uncle makes? I could eat a gallon of that."

"Yum," Liz said with a grimace. "Hope your dad is doing some of his grilled chicken that I can really go for." Uncle Zackery's sauce was too hot and spicy for Liz.

"Look ahead, see, there's the Miami skyline. I'll call Officer Hernandez and let him know we're almost there.

Chapter Seventy-Four

Officer Hernandez was a stocky Latino who met them in a security room at the terminal. His Cuban roots showed slightly in his pleasant accent.

The room was wall-to-wall CCTV computer screens set up to view much of the giant airport where over a thousand flights converged each day. Seth and Liz watched as officers sat scrolling, watching for Latimer.

Links to TSA for passenger control and Border and Customs could be accessed in seconds. A large map of the terminal dominated a screen behind Hernandez.

"We are monitoring incoming flights from China and Asia. If Latimer is meeting someone, we'll know about it." Hernandez said.

"We have officers patrolling the concourses looking for him. We are happy you offered to assist as you know the suspect and what he is capable of."

"What about the arrivals, air cargo and baggage areas?" Seth asked.

"We have that covered as well. I don't see how he could get past my men."

"Latimer is ruthless and clever. We don't know anything about this person he is meeting. It could even be another female." Liz said.

"I may be able to help there," Captain Jacobs said, entering the room. The captain handed one of the officers sitting at a computer a flash drive. The young officer plugged it in and pulled up the image and details of Michael Chang.

"I called in a couple favors, actually several favors from the State Department. You are looking at Michael Chang. He is a nephew of Daniel Chang, the head of the trafficking organization. Michael Chang and Meiling Chang grew up together and were taught their skills by masters in the deadly killing arts."

One of the officers alerted Hernandez to a plane landing from Singapore.

"I don't want any passenger to disembark from that plane," Hernandez shouted. "Get my people to the arrivals area quietly and see if they can spot Latimer waiting for Chang. Don't make a move until I say."

"You coming?" Hernandez said as he hurried down the hallway.

Seth, Liz, and Jacobs ran to keep up with Hernandez as he negotiated his way through the terminal to the gangway for the plane from Singapore. Armed security personnel were standing by, waiting for orders to board the plane.

"This is going to be difficult. Most of the passengers are Chinese or Japanese," Liz said.

Hernandez boarded the plane with two armed security agents. They went row by row, carefully inspecting passports. They let the elderly go first, along with women and children.

Liz watched, fascinated, as the single women came off next. Some women dressed in traditional Chinese attire, and some in up-market western clothes.

One woman caught her eye. The clothes didn't fit her body quite right. A flowing skirt flapped around her ankles, and a shawl covered part of her face, but she wore men's expensive leather shoes. Liz nudged Seth.

The woman rushed to the exit.

Without waiting, Seth took off after Chang, dressed as a woman, with Liz following.

Captain Jacobs radioed Officer Hernandez about Chang trying to flee the terminal.

Chang ran for the exit, but armed agents stood in his way. Ready to fight his way through, he stood poised to grab a passing teenage passenger, but Liz pushed the kid out of the way and offered herself up instead. The teen tumbled out of the way, shocked and scared.

"I'll make a much better hostage," Liz said. She stood just out of Chang's reach. As soon as Chang had his attention on Liz, reaching out to take her, Seth tackled him. Seth pulled the shawl over the man's head, temporarily blinding him.

"What the fuck," Chang yelled as he tried to untangle himself so he could see his assailant.

Seth brought Chang to the floor. Aware of Chang's skills, Liz jumped in and sat on Chang's legs so he couldn't dislodge Seth. Captain Jacobs and Officer Hernandez trotted up, and a dozen members of the Customs and Border Patrol team.

Tangled up in the shawl and the long skirt, Chang found himself cuffed and facing an assault rifle.

Officer Hernandez took the shawl off Chang's head. The man's eye glowed with venom. "Who do I have to thank for these?" shaking his cuffs.

"I guess that would be me, Florida Fish and Wildlife Commission Officer Seth Grayson, and my partner Officer Liz Corday."

"It figures. God damn FWC. Always screwing with our business," Chang spat out.

The officers took Chang away, walking him down the concourse to a door that said Security Only.

Hernandez slapped Seth on the back. "You and your partner make a hell of a good team."

"Yeah, I know," Seth said, embracing Liz and kissing her. "Don't you ever do anything like that again."

"What? I can't let you have all the fun."

"We are going to question Chang and see what he knows about Latimer and what he might be planning." Hernandez said following his men.

"You two got something I need to know about?" Captain Jacobs asked.

Chapter Seventy-Five

Latimer was in Baggage Claim waiting for Michael Chang when he began to hear rumblings from other arriving passengers about an arrest at one of the arrivals. He watched the passengers from the Singapore flight taking their luggage off the carousel but no word from Chang that he was on his way.

"Shit," Latimer mumbled as he watched the last bag circling the carousel. Looking at the name tag, it said simply Chang, no address. He dropped the bag and quickly looked for the exit.

"How the hell did they catch him?"

Latimer looked at the exit again. There was no way out that way. Armed security guarded the exit doors scrutinizing everyone leaving.

Thinking of going back into the terminal and looking for another way out, he saw more officers flowing into the baggage area. He panicked. It seemed like everyone watched him. More officers flowed into the baggage area. No way out there.

"Damn FWC," Latimer growled when he spied Liz and Seth, along with Captain Jacobs among them.

Frantically looking around, Latimer jumped on the moving carousel and rode it back into the baggage area.

"This way," Hernandez called, leading the way back to the handling area.

Latimer was running between the concourses, zigzagging

between planes. Seth and Liz didn't hesitate. They followed Latimer onto the tarmac.

He was dodging airport tugs that were towing trailers filled with baggage. He tried to run across the runway and was almost hit by an incoming plane, knocking over the marshal guiding the aircraft to its dock.

Latimer ran, trying to evade his pursuers by hiding in one of the baggage trailers that was headed back to the terminal.

The handlers tossed the baggage onto the conveyor that would take the bags to the carousel, exposing Latimer's hiding place.

Spotting their fugitive, Liz shouted, "There," taking off after Latimer.

Latimer drew his handgun and fired at Liz. "Latimer, there is no way out. Armed security is waiting for you. Give it up now." Liz shouted.

Latimer jumped on the conveyor belt and threw suitcases one after another at Seth and Liz.

Seth climbed on the conveyor, trying to get to Latimer before he reached the carousel and the opening to the main baggage claim area. That would put passengers waiting for their luggage in grave danger.

"Latimer, stop," Seth shouted. "This is going to end badly. Give it up."

Latimer raised his gun and fired. The shot echoed in the cavernous area.

Seth fell and fired back. Missing Latimer.

Liz watched a wet red stain spread over Seth's upper left chest below his shoulder.

"Son of a bitch." Liz fired, hitting Latimer twice in the chest. The trafficker went down. Liz had stopped him with a bullet that killed him instantly. The belt carried his body onto the carousel and out to the main baggage claim area.

Latimer's body, oozing blood, mixed with the baggage as Security rushed to the scene of screaming passengers waiting for their luggage.

Hernandez ordered the carousel shut down and the baggage

transferred to a different one.

"Cordon off this area," Hernandez shouted to his second in command. "Get a team in here to remove the body and see that Officer Grayson gets medical attention immediately. I want this place up and running as soon as possible."

Liz was sitting on the floor in the baggage loading area, holding Seth, pressing her hands to his wound trying to stop the blood slowly spreading across his shirt.

"Don't you dare die on me chief," Liz cried, tears running down her face. "Where's the damn ambulance?"

"It's on the way," Jacobs said as the siren's wail sounded.

Seth looked up at Liz, "I can't die. Remember I have to buy you that ten carat diamond."

"Screw the diamond. You're all that I need."

Chapter Seventy-Six

"Mom, you don't have to baby me. I can still feed and dress myself," Seth complained. His mother cut up his fried gator and poured some of his favorite Seminole Golden Barbecue Sauce on it.

"I will if I want to. My son is a hero and got shot." A tear escaped Rowena''s eyes and rolled down her wrinkled cheek.

"I'm proud of both of you," Andres said. "You have a dangerous job that most people don't appreciate."

"Thank you for that," Liz said between bits of the fried gator. "You know this stuff isn't half bad." Liz was trying everything on the menu at the big family gathering.

Seth's Uncle Zackery and the cousins had roasted a wild pig for the occasion and had cooked up some catfish, flounder, and fried gator tail. The women had provided all kinds of salads. Some were made with fresh vegetables and wild herbs grown in their own gardens.

Seth took Liz by the hand and whispered in her ear, "Come walk with me."

Hand and hand, they walked a path that led away from the picnic area and down to a small pond.

Beside the pond was a bench, like the one at the community center where his parents lived in Tampa. Seth sat and pulled Liz down beside him.

"You know, with me getting shot and both of us having to fill out statements, there is one thing we forgot to do," Seth said, rubbing his thumb over Liz's hand.

"I forgot too. We didn't have time to shop for the ten-carat diamond engagement ring." Liz reached up and caressed Seth's cheek, running her fingers over the scars from the snake bite he received in childhood.

"Well, while you were filling out your statement, which was longer than mine, I went shopping." Seth dug in his jeans pocket and pulled out a small blue velvet box. He got down on one knee and, facing Liz, opened the box.

"Elizabeth Corday, will you marry me…someday in the not-too-distant future?"

Liz looked at the sparkling one-carat diamond surrounded by a halo of smaller diamonds. She held her breath for a moment.

"It's perfect. How did you manage this?"

"Officer Hernandez knew a man who knew a man who owned a jewelry store. They kind of brought the store to me."

Seth slipped it on her finger. Liz held her hand out, admiring the ring. "It's perfect. Oh, Seth, yes, I want to marry you, and that sometime in the future may be closer than you think."

"Can we tell your mom and dad now, please?" she asked

Walking back to the gathering, everyone stopped talking and eating to look at them.

Seth and Liz stood confused, wondering what was going on until Seth's mom and dad started clapping, the tribe joined in drums, and music started.

Rowena rushed to hug Seth and Liz, smiling as she said, "It's about time. Now can I have grandkids?"

Acknowledgments

I have to thank my editor Mark Mathes for making this book the best it can be and my mentor DL Havlin for all his encouragement and advice over the years.

I need to mention Susan Klaus, a native Floridian, for some insight into old Florida. Her stories about how things used to be will stay with me always.

Excerpt from ABC News

By Julia Jacobo

October 20, 2019, 2:57 PM

Florida wildlife officials have uncovered a trafficking ring of thousands of smuggled turtles following a long-term undercover investigation.

Two suspects have been charged for poaching the turtles, most of them native to Florida, and selling them illegally, according to a news release by the Florida Fish and Wildlife Conservation Commission. Many of the turtles ended up in international markets, including those in Asia, officials said.

The FWC launched the investigation in February 2018 after receiving a tip from the public. Investigators determine that a "ring of well-organized wildlife traffickers" was catching and selling the turtles to large-scale reptile dealers and illegal distributors, who would then ship most of them overseas on the black market, according to the release.

One of the suspects, 39-year-old Fort Myers resident Michael Boesenberg, allegedly directed others to collect the turtles in "large numbers." Once they "had enough," they would then sell them to a buyer with links to Asian markets, FWC officials said.

The turtles were sold wholesale for up to $300 each and retailed for as much as $10,000 in Asia. In one month alone, an estimated $60,000 worth of turtles were trafficked out of Florida, according to the FWC

While the turtles were mostly sold for cash, the poachers would occasionally trade them for marijuana products, officials said.

The poachers would target habitats known for specific species of turtles and "depleted the species so much" that they had to expand to other parts of the state, according to the FWC. Lee County, the primary location of the poaching, was the most heavily impacted, but the effect on the wild turtle population overall stretched beyond the state.

"Wild turtle populations cannot sustain the level of harvest that took place here," said Dr. Brooke Talley, the Reptile and Amphibian Conservation Coordinator for the FWC. "This will likely have consequences for the entire ecosystem and is a detriment for our citizens and future generations."

Turtles are one of the most threatened animal groups on the planet, Dr. Craig Stanford, Chairman of the International Union for the Conservation of Nature's Tortoise and Freshwater Turtle Specialist Group, said in a statement.

"The illegal trade of turtles is having a global impact on many turtle species and our ecosystems," FWC Executive Director Eric Sutton said in a statement. "We commend our law enforcement's work to address the crisis of illegal wildlife trafficking."

More than 600 turtles were returned to the wild as a result of the investigation, and about half of those are now part of a long-term monitoring project by the Sanibel-Captiva Conservation Foundation, which has been conducting research on them for almost 20 years, officials said.

About the author

Brenda M. Spalding is a prolific award-winning author. A frequent speaker at writers' conferences and area writers' groups, where her knowledge of publishing and marketing is always welcome.

She is a past president of the National League of American Pen Women- Sarasota Branch, a member of the Sarasota Authors Connection, Sarasota Fiction Writers, Florida Authors and Publishers, and a co-founding member and current president of ABC Books Inc.

Her company, Braden River Consulting LLC, was formed to help other authors on their creative journey

www.bradenriverconsulting.com
www.brendaspaldingauthor.com
bradenriverconsulting@gmail.com
spaldingauthor@gmail.com

www.ingramcontent.com/pod-product-compliance
Lightning Source LLC
Chambersburg PA
CBHW070350200726
48294CB00003B/821